Boone:

The Ordinary

Claudia,
I pray that you will never be ordinary!

Blessings
Lauren H. Brandenburg ♡

Boone:

The Ordinary

Lauren H. Brandenburg

Illustrated by Jordan Crawford

KPP
KINGDOM PUBLISHING PRESS

This book my be ordered through booksellers or by contacting:

Kingdom Publishing Press
www.kingdompublishingpress.com

Or directly at the book series website:
Boone Tackett Series
www.boonetackett.com

Cover art by Jason Dudley

ISBN: 978-0-9896330-1-7

Library of Congress Control Number: 2012912991

Printed in the United States of America

For
Jamie, Kensi, and Jack

"For what you see and hear depends a great deal on where you are standing; it also depends on what sort of person you are."

C.S. Lewis
The Magicians Nephew

Chapter 1

Boone Tackett considered himself ordinary like everything that surrounded his ordinary life. Everyday was exactly uneventful, and he liked it that way. He woke to the sounds of the occasional scraping of spatula and sizzling of hot grease. "Just a little longer," he thought wiggling deeper into the warmth of his bed. "I can sleep five more minutes." Those five minutes turned into thirty and, once again, he knew that as usual he would be late for church. He pulled on his blue jeans and a wrinkled button down shirt, and ran his fingers through the curly black hair that was characteristic of the men on his father's side. Boone ran out the door, down the gravel driveway, and across the street to the church he had attended every Sunday since he was born.

Like most churches built in its day, it had a white steeple, was completely constructed of red brick and was adorned both top and bottom with stained glass windows. It quietly sat on the outskirts of town on a hill proudly overlooking acres of tobacco fields.

Boone slung open the basement door and breathed a sigh of relief at the sight of two lonely doughnuts that had been left in an open cardboard box in the church kitchen. On closer inspection, he frowned at the custard-filled confections wishing they were chocolate glazed, filled his glass with what was left of the juice, and snuck into an empty seat in the already occupied room designated "youth".

Boone lifted his brown eyes to look at the others sitting around the table and then down to the powdered sugar doughnut and half a cup of orange juice that comprised his breakfast. His stomach wished he had been up in time to eat his mom's traditional Sunday morning meal of scrambled eggs and bacon.

He raised his hand to his mouth to cover the escaping yawn, rubbed his eyes, and then allowed them to wander the perimeter of the concrete room. An autographed poster of the band Wet Feet, from last year's youth retreat, was the wall's sole decoration. He looked up at the cracked paint peeled ceiling and then tilted his head to get a better look at what he considered to be grape jelly oozing from a back corner. He shuddered at the thought of what it really might be.

The *tat a tat, tat a tat, tat a tat* of his cousin Case's fingers rhythmically drumming brought Boone's focus back to the group. Boone had never figured out how two people so closely related could look and exist so differently. Case was the complete opposite of Boone. His frame was tall and thin; a contrast to Boone's much shorter stature, and as perceived of most redheads, Case's skin was light and dotted with freckles - lots of freckles. Even though Case denied it, unlike Boone he was popular at school and was a great musician.

Boone sighed harder. Sunday after Sunday, he went. He sat, ate his doughnuts, and no matter how hard he tried, he could not get himself to focus on the lesson. "Boone? Are you with us?" the voice of Reed Hoffman, a volunteer youth leader in training, questioned. Suddenly, all eyes were on him, putting him somewhere he hated the most, the center of attention.

"What was the question?" Boone asked unsurely.

Reed rambled on as he unraveled the account of Eden life and Eve, aka the wife of Adam. All the while, he gave Boone the 'I can count on you' look that Boone had become accustomed to over the years of Sunday school lessons. Boone had literally grown up in church. Every major event in his life had found its way into this very building. His first step was taken during a Sunday night service during the singing of *Just As I Am*. His first tooth he lost while dressed as a donkey in the Christmas pageant, and his first girl friend, not to be confused with girlfriend, was Noel, the music leader's daughter. So for the past thirteen years of his life, every teacher he ever had depended on him to know the answers. Truth told, he thought that he did know all the answers.

Even though his juice was now warm, he tipped it up and chugged it anyway, spilling a few drops on his shirt. The juice gave him a quick burst of energy. He shook off his boredom, opened his eyes wide, and focused on Reed. Then it was gone. His attention lost again. Above him, Boone heard the rattle and raking of the heating system struggling in determination to knock the morning chill off those below. A flash of hot air poured down, wrapping him in a blanket of warmth and lulling him into sleepiness. His eyelids grew heavy and finally fell closed with relief. The damp smell of slightly moist carpet filled his nostrils as very vivid images of a man and woman working in an exotic garden scurried around in his brain.

Boone jerked himself awake. Then he went back to allowing his eyes to wander. Occasionally, he nodded his head as if he were actually listening to the college student explain the fall of man. A quick kick to his right shin sent pain up his leg. With her hazel green eyes glaring, Noel Peterson gave him a jolting reminder that she was sitting directly across from him and that he should be paying attention. She eased her glower, replaced it with a quick smile, and motioned to her left. Feet propped on the folding table, legs outstretched, arms crossed across his chest, and eyes closed were a clear indication that Wayne Adams had fallen asleep, again. Boone covered his mouth to hold in his laughter, but it wasn't enough to contain the rumbling. Deep from within his belly, the grandfather of all laughs emerged, stopping Reed on the word 'forbidden' and sending Wayne and all his lankiness flying backwards in his seat. The metal folding chair clanged shut as the class of eight erupted in hysterics. Boone knew an apology would be in order, but before he had time the distorted *BZZZZSCHRING* of a cracked bell announced the end of Sunday school.

"Don't forget, 6:00, Wednesday!" Reed called to the escaping teens while stifling his own laughter. "Sit on the front row…that means you too Wayne!" Boone led the exodus of exiting teens. He glimpsed back briefly to see if Noel had finished collecting her Bible and journal into the trendy quilted backpack that she carried everywhere. He actually thought the pink and green floral contraption was completely ugly, but knew telling her would mean that he would have to see her girlie emotional side. That was something he had never seen in the three years they had been friends, and never wanted to see. He waited outside the room for her. Wayne and Case stood close by punching each other in the arm to see who could hit the hardest. The act had become a post class ritual for them, however neither was ever declared the winner. Upon her appearance, the group made their way up the back staircase that led into the sanctuary of the Great Crossing Baptist Church.

Boone stopped at the top step and took a deep breath. He knew that he had one more hour ahead of him before he could return to the comfort of his bed. He turned the corner and took in what he accepted to be the extreme ordinariness of his childhood place of worship. The church was old, not old like his grandmother or even his great grandmother, but really old, like established in 1785 old. It was the oldest church in their small town and very unlike the newer churches in nearby towns with fancy lighting, stadium seating, and a band complete with backup singers and a drum cage. The people at Great Crossing still sat in long wooden pews that lined perfectly into two rows, with an aisle cascading down the center towards the front of the sanctuary. An enormous brass chandelier that hung high above lighted the two-story room, and most of the music was still accompanied by an organ. The crew picked up their pace when a second bell rang announcing a five-minute warning that worship would begin soon.

Members were already seated in the pews reading the church bulletin, and casually chatting with one another about the potential success of the high school basketball team or how crops were going to do this year. Boone had heard these conversations many times and moved forward with hands in his pockets thinking that maybe someone would say something different for once. His eyes studied the movement of his brown leather flip-flops as they moved across the velvety floor beneath him.

"Hey Pinky!" Wayne jeered up to Noel, who was already turning the corner into the red-carpeted room. "Why'd you have to go and ruin my nap?" Case snickered at the comment wanting to be in on torturing Noel. They liked her, but didn't like how close she had become to Boone, nor could they understand why he was friends with a girl. They took every available opportunity to point out the prissy things she did that detracted from her occasional tomboyish manner.

"Last summer guys! Really, let it go," she smartly called back to them without turning her head. Noel didn't want to give them the satisfaction of seeing the flush of her cheeks. Boone knew they wouldn't let it go. Her scientifically, and partially curiosity driven hair experiment with a bottle of lemon juice and hydrogen peroxide would never be forgotten. "Oh, and it wasn't really pink, more like orange. You know, like yours Case," she laughed trying not to let them get the better of her. Noel's father had been leading the music for three years now. To the boys, she was still the new girl. To Boone, she was his very best friend. She wasn't like any other girl he had ever met. She didn't like to wear dresses. She never wore make-up, and her mousy brown hair was always pulled into a ponytail. She was smart and Boone could count on her to take on whatever adventure he could conjure up, no matter how muddy.

5

"Okay Pinky," Wayne coughed under his breath. Case snickered. Noel rolled her eyes. Boone knew the comment was meant more for him and Case than Noel. If Wayne could make anyone laugh at anything, then he had accomplished his goal for the day. Right now, Wayne was silently declaring victory.

"Why do we always have to sit in the front?" Case moaned walking three steps behind the others.

"It sends a message," Noel replied. "One, it says to the older people that we are an important part of the church. And two, it says we have to be good. If not, someone in the choir will tell our parents." Boone hoped she would stop there, but he knew her well and he knew she wouldn't. "Besides, this is a little church compared to most of the ones I have been to. It's easier for our actions to be more closely observed. If we were a bigger group like…"

Case cut her off. "We know! Everything was awesome there; the youth group was *so* big." He put his pointer finger to his mouth and pretended to gag himself. She ignored him. Her parents couldn't have plopped Noel down in a place more opposite from where she had grown up. Before her move, she had attended a prestigious private school where most of her friends were also a part of her church youth group. Her youth group had had a funny name like *Explosion* or *Experience*. Boone could never remember which it was. At Great Crossing they were simply called the youth group.

They filed into the unoccupied second row of the crimson padded white pews. As always, they were in the same order. Wayne sat on the end, Case to his left, followed by Boone, and then Noel - until Kaylee made her way in. Boone hated having his six-year-old sister Kaylee sit with them. He had fought that battle with his parents only once.

"She's not even kind of close to being a youth yet!" he had argued.

"Boone," his mother had come back in her teachable moment voice, "this is a good time for you to be an example. She doesn't want to sit with you anyway. She wants to sit by Noel."

6

That was the end of the argument. He knew better than to ask a second time. Kaylee took her place as the bookend at the very end of the row.

Noel's dad entered the room of patient patrons, followed by a choir clothed in scarlet robes. The gold-toned cross that hung above the built-in baptistery was quickly concealed by their presence. His cool voice welcomed everyone to the service. With authority, he raised both arms in the air signaling the congregation to stand. Boone stood as everyone around him joined together in singing the first and third verses of *Amazing Grace*, but was distracted as usual. He squinted to interpret the church attendance board that hung over the piano. "Fifty-three in Sunday school," he added. "We're down two from last week." That was one of the first major church differences Noel had pointed out, the attendance board.

"Seriously, why does everyone need to know how many are in Sunday school?" Noel had questioned. "Is there a prize or something?" He hadn't wanted to share with her that yep, there actually was a Sunday where they gave out prizes for high attendance. He had guessed by her tone that was something they had not done at her previous church, and then later learned that she didn't even have Sunday school before moving.

His boredom took him to the clock on the right of the sanctuary. "Urgh," he silently grumbled, "forty-five more minutes to go." The congregation was starting their second song. It was a new song with a more contemporary beat that Noel's dad had brought to the service. At first it wasn't accepted very well seeing as how it wasn't in the cloth bound hymnal. But recently, he could tell by participation that it had become a congregational favorite. Mr. Peterson raised his arms again and then slowly lowered them, signaling that everyone could be seated. Papers crumbled, hymns were shut, and a contagion of rear ends taking their seat on squeaky benches followed. Boone sat, and then jumped up realizing that he had almost squashed the contents of Noel's backpack. "Sorry," he apologized.

She smiled, pulled it out of his way, and set it precisely at her feet. As she sat, Jeff Morgan handed her a neatly folded piece of paper. Boone waited for the blond-headed preacher's kid to turn back around on the front row. "What's that?" he asked curiously.

"I don't know," she said keeping her voice low.

"Open it!" Boone quietly begged.

"No!"

"Why not?" he asked, now even more curious.

"Because it's private," she teased.

Private, Boone thought. *Private?* They didn't have secrets between them. He didn't like it. Actually, he really didn't even like Jeff. Jeff had been around the church as long as Boone. His mom was a local first grade teacher, his grandmother was the church organist, and his dad had been the preacher for the last seven years. Boone could never really pinpoint what it was that he didn't like about Jeff. Jeff was smart, athletic, and all the kids at school really liked him. He was nice to everyone, especially Noel. But for some reason, he and Boone had never gotten along. Even as toddlers in the nursery, they didn't play together. So the pocket-sized piece of paper that Noel hid deep within her backpack was doing its job of irritating Boone.

"Read it," Boone whispered to her, catching the eye of Pastor Morgan who was now is position to preach his sermon.

"No Boone!" she insisted showing that she was becoming frustrated.

"Noel…" The sharp tug on the back of his ear silenced him. He shot around to see his Aunt Carter holding her finger to her puckered lips. Boone turned, slouched down in the pew, and crossed his arms in front of his chest. He tried to focus on the enthusiastic words of Pastor Morgan, but his mind wandered. He planned to continue this conversation with Noel immediately after the service.

The early October sunlight streamed through the rectangular stained glass windows that lined both the up and downstairs of the sanctuary. There were sixteen total, four on each side of the lower portion of the room and four on each side of the church's balcony. Boone knew that there were sixteen. He had counted them during many services, as he had also counted the number of light bulbs in the chandelier, the number of people in the choir, and sometimes the number of times Pastor Morgan called out, "Can I get an amen?" in a single service. Today, he was up to five. The sunlight became more intense, tossing a rainbow of colors across the white plaster walls. Boone glanced downward as a speck of red light found its way to the back of his hand.

His curiosity followed the light up to its home on the far side of the church. Behind the iron balcony railing, Boone watched as the beam of light rested beside a beehive of glass. Then, it jumped to the illustration of an open Bible, inlaid in blue glass and encircled by deep red. The light grew brighter and more intense. He tried to blink, but his eyes would not shut. At the bottom of the window inset in its own pane of glass were the words "To him that worketh not." In thirteen years, he had never seen those words.

He read them under his breath, "To him that worketh not." The light from the chandelier began to flash off and on. Silence filled the room. Pastor Morgan's mouth still moved and his hands still gestured, but Boone couldn't hear what he was saying. The flickering of the grand light fixture increased. "Is this a joke?" he questioned nervously noticing that no one moved from their seat to fix the malfunction above them. Then, the carpet pulled up from the floor sending tacks flying through the air. The paint chipped off the walls raining flecks of white over the unmoving churchgoers. With a horrible untamed howl the organ played uncontrollably. Boone hurriedly scanned the room, looking side to side for anyone in any way acknowledging this event. With a loud pop, the flashing ended and everything returned as it was. Once again, Boone could hear the words of Jeff's father.

"Noel," Boone whispered, "did you see that?"

"Hush, Boone," she warned.

Boone laid his head back against the pew and peered over at the stained glass window. He wished he had just stayed in bed. Things like this didn't happen to him. He gulped, "This is definitely not ordinary."

Chapter 2

"Who eats green beans with pizza?" Boone groaned at
the meal in front of him. He carried his plastic orange tray to one
of the many long tables in the middle school cafeteria and placed
it beside Wayne's. Lunch was usually Boone's favorite hour of the
day. However today he imagined that if he closed his eyes for
even a second he would find his face planted in a patch of
mozzarella and tomato sauce.

He had been up most of the night recounting the events
of the prior morning. Boone knew he hadn't been seeing things,
but was not completely certain that it wasn't some a joke meant
solely for him. His first assumption was that Reed was using
some kind of college level subliminal mind trick on him as
payback for interrupting the class. He almost believed that was
the absurd explanation, but in the minutes where he had drifted
off to sleep, he was awakened by a loud *pop*, finding that he was
covered in sweat and thinking about those words. It was the
words that freaked him the most, 'him that worketh not.' Boone

11

couldn't stop thinking about them and why he had never paid attention to them before.

"You gwana eat fwose?" Wayne asked with a mouth full of pizza and pointing to Boone's uneaten beans.

"Um, no," Boone answered pushing the tray towards him, but grabbing his pizza first. He was worn out, but he could always eat. The cafeteria bustled with the noise of hungry teens, clanging silverware, and crashing trays. At the far end of the room, a longer table stretched perpendicular to the student tables. A row of teachers sat there eating their tuna fish sandwiches and drinking diet sodas. Occasionally, one of them would stand and pass a glare over the room to make sure that mashed potatoes were not flying through the air or a sixth grader wasn't being tortured.

After a few seconds of sitting on the attached bench, Boone realized that the other two weren't there. "Where's Case?" he asked interrupting Wayne's chewing.

Wayne coughed and swallowed hard as he gulped down some white milk. "Assembly."

Boone grinned, remembering the reason he purposefully had chosen to not finish his Language Arts homework. On any other day, the idea of not finishing Ms. Shelly's writing assignment wouldn't have crossed his mind. He had a love hate relationship with the class. Actually, it was more like a love scared to death relationship with it. Boone loved the class and how he was encouraged to be creative and be himself, but he was absolutely petrified of the woman that taught it. She was the most intelligent woman he had ever known, and Boone felt like she could see right through him, right to the chunk of him that begged, "Please don't call on me! Please don't call on me!" Her grey eyes would stare a person down. And with that stare, she knew instantly whether or not you had completed her work. The thought of her gave Boone shivers.

But today, there was an assembly. The gathering of students was to take place right after lunch at exactly the same time as eighth grade Language Arts. Boone figured he had one more day to finish the weekend assignment. "I was up all night," Noel stated taking her usual place across from Boone with her packed lunch in hand.

"Me too," Boone remarked consuming his first bite of the greasy goodness.

"So what did you write about?" she innocently questioned as she squeezed open her carton of lemonade.

"Nothing," Boone yawned.

She stared him in the eye. "Boone, tell me you finished your homework. She told us we had to turn it in sometime today before the assembly!"

Boone started to feel his lunch churning in his stomach. He couldn't think. His first quarter report card loudly proclaimed to his parents a giant C minus. He had been warned that if he didn't bring it up by the end of term he would be grounded during fall break. Boone thought fast. He reached into his three-ring binder for a blank sheet of loose-leaf notebook paper. "Something is better than nothing," he rationalized.

Boone dug into the back pocket of his jeans for a pencil with no luck. There wasn't much time left in lunch and he had to at least start his personal narrative assignment. At that moment, the figure of a woman dressed in a pale blue suit jacket and skirt stood up to take her turn at policing the room. It was her! Boone looked away to avoid meeting her glare. Out of the corner of his eye he could see her looking his way. *She knows*, he worried.

Slowly, he turned his back to the woman and hunched over his blank paper. He peeked sideways to Noel for help, but found her laughing hysterically and struggling to contain the chocolate chip cookie in her mouth. "You totally believed me," she giggled.

"What?" he asked confused.

"You're too easy today! Boone, what's up?"

Boone's lips parted into a half smile. "Ha, ha, you're funny," he said still feeling the stress of what it would have been like to face Sheila Shelly empty handed.

"Oh," Noel stated staring hard at her friend, "heard about your nightmare in Science this morning."

"Nice," Boone mumbled. Word had traveled fast and by now everyone in the whole school knew what had happened an hour earlier. A bee had landed on the classroom windowsill outside. He had observed it buzzing and bouncing seeking to find a way in. Boone remembered the beehive in the stained glass at church, wondering if this bee lived in a similar hive. His musings had carried into his imaginary beehive where all the bees oddly resembled people from the church. There he became caught up in the busyness of the bees flying in and out. The buzzing of the bees had grown so loud in his head that he stood up in the middle of class, clasped his hands over his ears, shouted "STOP", and in doing so sent his science book flying at Makayla Beckett giving her a bloody nose.

The slow *ding, ding, ding* of the schools digital bell system announced the end of lunch and a four minute travel time to get to the assembly. Wayne, Noel, and Boone gathered their trash, tossed it in the appropriate recycling bins, and made their way through herds of students to the already crowded gymnasium.

The wooden bleachers had been pulled out from the sidewalls to seat the mass of middle school students. The smell of sweat still lingered in the air from earlier P.E. classes. Noel hurriedly took her seat. "I'm so excited!" she proclaimed.

"Seriously?" Wayne questioned while folding his homework into various right angles.

Boone had to admit that assemblies were a nice change from the day to day, but he was certain that he wasn't going to enjoy an hour focused entirely on the town's history. This was nothing new to him. But Noel, who hadn't grown up being submerged in the many civic traditions that surrounded them, had managed to miss the opening assembly for Founder's Week the past two years and saw this as something interesting.

The 7th and 8th grade choir noisily filed onto the risers positioned on the stage at the back of the gym. Dressed in yellow and green striped collared shirts, they were a patriotic display of the school colors. On the back row, Case Carter's red hair glowed under the spotlighting. He was a statue, arms down to his side, and eyes focused on Mr. Paris the choir director. With a hushed, "One, two, three," the balding man brought the young voices together in unison.

"*The sun shines bright,*" they sang holding out the last note for a few seconds before moving on to the words, "*on my old Kentucky home.*" Case's trained tenor voice rose above the rest. Boone often forgot how good he really was.

"Why doesn't he ever sing in church?" Noel asked still listening intently. "He really should, you know."

"He's way too cool for us," Boone mocked.

"Have *you* ever asked him?" she questioned, emphasizing the word 'you'.

"No, but it wouldn't matter. He wouldn't listen to me."

"Are you kidding? He and Wayne do everything you say. You have to know that!"

Boone didn't know that. He hesitated a minute and decided to change the subject. "What was that paper all about that Jeff gave you yesterday?"

She took her focus off the choir and looked into Boone's brown eyes. "Like I said, it's private."

"Private?" he wondered. "What does that even mean?"

"Boone, I'm joking! It was something about Wednesday night youth group. It's not a big deal."

"Oh," Boone mouthed, still not completely understanding. The choir ended their tribute by raising their right arms slowly in the air and bowing. The students enthusiastically clapped their hands and stomped their feet, solely for creating a thunderous echo that bounced off the high walls. Meanwhile, the choir exited the stage row by row.

"All right, all right! Calm down," the raspy female voice of Mrs. Stout, the school principal, projected through the microphone. "Otherwise, we can all go back to class and do more work." Boone knew this was just a threat repeated at every assembly; it had never actually been done. With her mouth so close to the microphone that it produced an occasional squeal, the principal continued, "It is my privilege, in honor of Founder's Week," she cleared her throat and brushed a gray hair from the front of her violet rimmed glasses, "to welcome back, all the way from the 1700's, one of our proud founders, the Reverend Elijah Craig!" The stomping and cheering began again, but was abruptly silenced by the two-finger whistle of Ms. Shelly.

A statuesque man dressed in a black suit with high collar and ruffled shirt sauntered to the center of the stage. He silently observed with his large dark eyes first the students sitting on the right, then those sitting on the left. He glanced hazily upward toward the scoreboard, and then down to the glossy wood floors below. His thin pale hand reached into his coat and removed a pocket watch. He took a quick look at it and then put it back where it had once rested. "What an amazing structure this is," he spoke with a drawl that was thick and Southern. "I must say - this is strange. You know, I believe that this building could be constructed on the very land I purchased back in 1782." Boone, unlike Noel who was immersed in the town history about to be unraveled before her, was bored. He had heard this story so many times he could recite it from memory. "I was born in Virginia, but followed the Traveling Church of 600 over the mountains in 1781 after my brothers and their families."

His boredom led him to scan the room. He watched as kids whispered with one another, passed notes, or doodled on the back of their notebooks. Wayne's disinterest in the program was evident by the finishing touches he was putting on his Chinese throwing star. Even the teachers weren't paying attention. A few sat against the back wall grading papers, and a select group paced the room monitoring the behavior of their classes. On the opposite side of the gymnasium, Boone's lack of interest changed to curiosity at the sight of an elderly man wearing a wide brimmed straw hat. The unfamiliar man listened keenly as the speaker boasted about his character's many accomplishments. *Maybe somebody brought their papaw*, Boone thought. Then as if on cue, the man stood up and smiled at Boone. He raised his left hand in a slight waving gesture and then sat back down. Boone looked around to see if maybe someone behind him was waving, but no one was paying attention. When he turned back, the strange man was gone.

"I preached at several churches and then became the pastor of a smaller church not too far from here. I believe that church is still around today." The man disguising himself as the 18th century reverend continued, "But you already knew that, didn't you, Boone Tackett?"

The lights flashed as they had done the morning before in church. An unusual sickness came over him that made him lightheaded and nauseous. He was stunned to see that the students around him were frozen in their acts of not paying attention. Wayne was in position to throw his handmade star and Noel had pencil in hand ready to take notes on the presentation. Even the large window mounted fans that were cooling the warm October day were caught mid-spin. Boone tried to stand, but his legs were wobbly and weak. The lights went dark, except for the one spotlight still shining brightly on the resemblance of Elijah Craig.

"You know all about me, don't you Mr. Tackett?" the reverend questioned. Boone remained perfectly still trying to balance on his unsteady legs. "You were born here. You have heard the tale many times. You know all about the Mishpachah. Or at least you think you do. Isn't that right?"

Boone opened his mouth to speak, but deduced that this was another daydream, and he was going to wake up any minute. He pinched the back of his hand hard. "Wake up, wake up!" he told himself.

"It is polite to answer your elders, son. Tell me, what do you know about the Mishpachah?" Elijah Craig inquired again.

"I, um, I," Boone stuttered. "It's only a story, a fairy tale, from when I was a kid."

"Ha, ha, ha," the man chuckled. "Oh to him that worketh not."

A hand rested on Boone's back. Boone jerked around to see the man in the wide brimmed hat looking at him smiling; his silver blue eyes sparkled with certainty. They were alone now, no students, no teachers. Even Elijah Craig had vanished. Any fear that Boone had disappeared with everyone else, as if the stranger's presence had instantly drawn it out of him. The elderly man closed his eyes and then opened them. "You are him," he stated assuredly.

Boone didn't want to move. He opened his mouth to speak, but the questions he had wouldn't come out. The man took his hand from Boone's back and placed it over Boone's weary eyes, closing them gently. Boone could feel the calluses of the man's fingertips on his face. He could smell the scent of earthiness that brought to memory summers picking beans in his grandmother's garden.

He breathed in deep and opened his eyes. Noel sat vigorously writing down every word the man spoke. Wayne was beginning construction on another paper weapon. The teachers were still watching and grading. The representation of the reverend had returned to the stage. His arms were now folded proudly across his chest and with his chin raised high he continued. "Prosperous? Oh yes." His speech became solemn, "I was quite the business man. I built the first mill for cloth manufacturing in the state and even founded a school. But there are those that say I sold out to the world. The more I tried to carry through with my plans, the poorer I became." The gymnasium was silent now except for the *whoosh whoosh* of the fans. Everyone knew what was coming next.

"What's going on?" Noel asked.

"This is when he talks about the Mishpachah," Boone stammered feeling numb and confused.

"The what?" Noel asked.

"Shhhhhh," those around her demanded.

The Elijah Craig imitator sauntered to the edge of the stage. "But what really happened is that I found happiness in something else, something so mysterious that it was hidden from the rest of the world..."

Ding, Ding, Ding. The school bell caught the students off guard, calling to their attention the end of the school day. Backpacks were hastily gathered together as students briskly scrambled to exits. On stage, the slender frame of the man bowed at the waist, his arms hung down by his sides, and his head dropped forward. He raised himself up, and then he flopped over again, bobbing up and down like a worm on a hook. "Do not clap for me, but for our founder, the Reverend Elijah Craig," he shouted over the confusion of scattering students.

"What!" Noel jumped to her feet. "That's it? What about that Mishpachah thing?"

Boone smiled at her excitement. "It's a story. We've all heard it since we were kids. It's not a big deal."

"Not a big deal! Everyone acted like he was going to tell them where to find free money! There has to be more to it," she insisted slinging her backpack over her shoulder and placing her hands on her hips.

Boone started to change the subject again, but was interrupted by a *WHAP* and a sudden stinging sensation on the back of his head. He looked down to see that Wayne's star was resting at his feet. Boone reached forward, picked it up, and turned to fling it at its owner, but stopped abruptly finding himself face to face with Ms. Shelly.

Her eyes were reading him. "Are you him?" she asked.

The lights weren't flashing and people were moving. "I'm sorry ma'am. What was the question?" She terrified him.

"Are you him?" she asked again. Boone was about to answer when she asked in a tone of clear authority, "Does this folded piece of origami belong to you?"

With relief he answered, "No ma'am."

"Thank you, Mr. Tackett," she said turning to walk away, but then she stopped. Ms. Shelly turned back and stated accusingly, "Don't you ever try to cheapen your writing by doing it at the lunch room table. Is that understood? You have potential. Don't ruin it by making a selfish mistake."

"Yes ma'am," he answered not wanting to blink or take his eyes off her until she was out of sight.

Boone didn't understand why all of the peculiar things were happening to him, but whatever it was, he had decided that he had better keep it to himself. The last thing he wanted right now was for his friends to find out that he was going mad.

Chapter 3

Rain trickled down the windows of the Tackett's outdated mini-van as it cruised past miles of limestone walls. The rock fences gave way to a series of old homes perched on the hilltops, looking down to the busy roadway below them. Seconds later, the family vehicle was in the heart of the downtown area. Coffee shops sat alongside antique vendors, intermingled with the occasional dentist or local real estate company. Boone crossed his arms and laid his head against the headrest. Another night of tossing and bizarre dreams had left him groggy and moody. His sister Kaylee sat in the captain's seat beside him methodically brushing the synthetic hair of her doll. Her sequined t-shirt sparkled in the periodic light that flickered through the windows from the street lamps outside. As always, her dark hair was neatly fixed, glitter was splattered across her cheeks, and her thin lips glistened with very berry lip-gloss. "Aren't you kind of young to be wearing makeup?" Boone taunted, feeling the sudden desire to pick a fight.

"It's not makeup, Boone," she said scowling at him. "It's lip GLOSS!"

He leaned in close to her and whispered, "You know what they make that stuff out of, don't you?"

"What?" she asked whimpering.

Mrs. Tackett whipped her head around to frown at Boone, "Not now, Boone." He sat back again in his seat fighting the urge to close his eyes. "Is everything okay at school?"

Her question caught him by surprise. "Sure, it's fine."

Mrs. Tackett turned back around in her seat. "You seem a little off lately. Is there anything you need to talk about?"

Boone considered it for a moment. How could he tell his parents that for the past three days he had been seeing people that weren't there, having nightmares, and hearing voices? He was sure they would either not believe him or have him committed to a hospital for the mentally ill. "Nope," he replied honestly and turned his attention to the evening rain falling outside.

The Tacketts passed the brick entrance to the town's college, reminding him of the rumors that also surrounded it and Elijah Craig. Boone wished he had never heard that name. Noel had bugged him all day about the Mishpachah, but he hadn't wanted to talk about it. "Ask Case," he had suggested, "or anyone. Everyone around here knows the story."

Noel's family lived in the historic area of town. He had been there so many times that he had lost count. The tan brick of the familiar Peterson's home was now visible. Their house was taller than those around it and sat on the corner of a busy four way stop. In the past years, her parents had spent all of their free time restoring the antique to its original state. The posts and detailed trim of the front porch were freshly painted white. Its light welcomed the guests and illuminated the porch swing and the girl that sat there reading with her legs folded underneath her. The van had barely stopped when Noel jumped up from her seat, slid open the van door, and grabbed Boone by the arm.

"I have something to tell you," her voice was hushed and hurried.

"Oh!" he stammered in surprise. Inside, a large staircase framed the left side of the home's foyer. It shot up and then made a ninety-degree turn to the right. Directly across from the front door was the family piano. At the bottom of the stairs was a lace covered round table. On it sat a lamp and Noel's great grandmother's Bible.

"Well, hello Boone," Mr. Peterson greeted him. "I'm glad your mom and dad brought you along. Noel mentioned that you had a project you were working on." Boone grinned at Noel knowing that there was no project. He pondered whether or not to go along with it or pay Noel back for her homework prank in the cafeteria the day before.

Her eyes were pleading, "Please go along with it!" He gave her a really big grin and tried hard to come up with something sarcastic to say.

"Our meeting shouldn't take long," Boone's dad announced while shaking the water off of his umbrella at the front door. "We'll have the homecoming service planned in no time."

"I can hardly believe it's that time of year again!" Boone's mom squealed, gently hugging Mrs. Peterson.

"It's a big one! Eighty-five years!" A much older version of Noel smiled back. Noel clutched Boone's arm once again and led him up the stairs as the parents gathered into the living room to organize the events of the yearly celebration of the church's history. Boone didn't understand why they were meeting to plan the event that was held in the exact same way every year. The morning would begin with the traditional service. A couple of people would stand up and say some nice things about the church. Prizes were given for the oldest member and the newest. Then everyone gathers in the parking lot afterward for a fish fry and potluck dinner. Boone actually looked forward to this day, mostly because of the vast assortment of pies and chocolate desserts that were brought in by the senior ladies of the church.

Noel resumed her grip on Boone's arm nearly dragging him up the stairs. At the top of the long staircase, two doors stood open and a third closed. Boone stopped and looked at Noel, "What are you doing? You're not allowed to have boys in your room! Your dad will never let me speak to you again!" Noel's dad had very strict rules about who was and was not allowed in her bedroom, and Boone was not one of them.

"We're not going to my room," she said as if he should have known. "We're going to the attic."

"The attic! Cool!" Boone exclaimed.

"Come on! Before your sister follows." Noel bounced over to the closed door at their left. She turned the old metal handle quietly and hurried him in. The room was filled with shelving that housed records, old cassette tapes, and CD's. A music stand was in the middle of the room with pages of sheet music neatly stacked on its ledge. At its base, a saxophone rested on its stand. The walls were dotted with framed pictures of Noel's dad posing with various choirs. Boone took a minute to walk the perimeter of the room and study each photograph. He stopped to look closely at one of a very large choir.

There wasn't much that Boone knew about the city where Noel was from. However, what he did know was that her parents had moved here for a change of pace and that she had begged them to let her stay behind. He wondered if this was a picture from that unknown place. Boone aimlessly investigated the room when a large object rammed into his side. Pain shot from one hip to the other. Noel's father's keyboard rocked helplessly back and forth on its stand. Noel lunged for the electric piano like a giant rubber band waiting to snap back. In the meantime, a stunned Boone stood agonizing. Noel was now leaning forward with one foot on the ground and another in the air. Her hands clutched the instrument for fear of it falling to the ground. Boone couldn't hold it in any longer. He fell on the floor rolling with laughter at the absurd sight of her tangled body. It made his side hurt even more, but he couldn't stop.

She glared down at him; her body still contorted. "If this falls and breaks, I'm telling my dad that you did it!"

"You wouldn't break your dad's keyboard...would you?"

24

"Try me," she threatened. Boone stared into her eyes, their gazes locked as if preparing to draw guns in an old Western movie. She moved one hand. He couldn't believe what she was about to do. "Are you done?"

Boone managed to get to his feet and shook his head. This time it was Noel who broke out in laughter. "What!" he cried realizing he had been outwitted.

"Boone, whatever is going on with you, you are almost no fun," she claimed trying to steady the piano. Noel moved to where a door seemed to be decoratively hanging on the wall a few feet from the floor. She opened it, braced herself, and then stepped up into the stairwell that the opened door revealed. "Are you coming?"

Boone's mouth hung open. Inside the door was a steep and very narrow staircase. There was no handrail and the wood plank walls were high. A warm breeze floated toward them and filled Boone's nostrils with the old mustiness from the room above. "What is this?"

"It's the attic! Isn't it great?" Noel beamed.

"Yes!" he said with anticipation of adventure. He was excited to see what was up there. The higher Boone went up the stairs, the darker it got. He glanced back to where he had started and then turned to make his way to the top. A soft *click click* filled the room with light and a blast of even warmer air covered him.

"Over here!" Noel called to him. The room was as large as the surface of the entire home. Labeled boxes were scattered all around, clothing racks were full of forgotten hanging items, and discarded pieces of furniture were pushed against the vaulted walls never to be used again. "Watch your head!" Boone looked up to see that the nails that secured the roofing shingles outside were protruding sharply through the wood panels on the ceiling.

In the far left corner of the space, Boone stepped over stacks of books to find Noel sitting on the floor. "Dad never said anything about having boys above my room!"

"Your room is underneath us?" he asked pointing to the bowing and dust covered wood floor.

"Right below," she smiled. Boone had an eerie feeling of being suspended in mid air. He figured he had to be at least thirty feet off the ground. "So daydreamer, spill it! What's going on?"

"Nothing!"

"Oh come on! You are acting really out of the ordinary lately. Not exactly the Boone Tackett that I know…why all the secrets and seriousness?"

"Secrets?" He hadn't thought about all the weirdness surrounding him as secrets. It was something he had kept private between him and his sanity. In his brain, she was the one with the secret.

"Why wouldn't you tell me about this mysterious Mishpachah thing?" she interrogated.

"I don't know. It's a stupid fairy tale, it's not important," he muttered. He was absolutely afraid that he might start seeing things again if he talked about it.

"Boone, it's important to me! Please, PLEASE!"

"Wait, you said you had something *really* important to tell me!"

"I do, but I want you to tell me the story first. Come on Boone," she begged.

"Alright, alright!" he gave in. Boone cleared his throat and began speaking in a high-pitched shaky exaggeration of the elderly, "Once upon a time…"

"Be serious, Boone!"

"Seriously, the story starts with 'once upon a time'. That's how everyone tells it. So do you want me to finish or not?" he asked.

"Fine, but don't use the granny voice."

"Okay…Once upon a time, there was a man by the name of Elijah Craig who founded a small town. He built a church, a school, and many businesses to grow the little village. At first, his businesses made him very wealthy and he wanted more. But soon, he found the more he tried to do the poorer he was becoming. So he asked God what he should do, and the Lord told him to give the fortune away. 'How much?' Mr. Craig had asked the Lord. 'All of it!' the Lord had replied. 'To whom shall I give it?' the preacher asked. 'The bride,' the Lord had answered. Being a preacher and a man of God's word, he knew that the Bible talked about the church being the bride of God's only son. So he gave all of his money to a church where he had once preached," Boone paused seeing that Noel was intrigued. "This is the part kids usually get excited about: Well, Elijah Craig thought that he would once again become wealthy because he had done what the Lord had told him and given all his riches to the church. But a month went by and he hadn't made any money. Then two months went by and nothing. Finally, on the seventh day of the seventh month, he went back to the church and sat underneath a tree on the church grounds. He pleaded with the Lord and begged Him for an answer, but the Lord was silent. Every month on the seventh day, he would return to that tree and pray. Each time he prayed and pleaded for the wisdom and wealth of Solomon, but as the months passed his heart changed. He no longer desired the wealth he had once known because he had learned to live without it. One day, his prayer changed as well, and he asked the Lord for the heart of David and the faith of Job. It was during this prayer that the ground opened up in front of him. Elijah Craig climbed down into the opening and the darkness engulfed him. On faith, he walked forward following the sound of water until suddenly before his very eyes…" Boone stopped.

"Why did you stop? What happened? What did he see? Was it God?" Noel asked feverishly.

If Boone had water in his mouth, he would have spewed it out. "No it wasn't God! It was the Mishpachah!"

"Oh. Keep going!"

"Okay…so, right before his very eyes was the most beautiful land he had ever seen. It was an amazing display of silver waterfalls and emerald gardens. It was a place that sparkled with diamond dust and dripped with gold. It was wealth beyond the imagination. But no one really knows what happened to him. Some say Mr. Craig died that very day under the old tree. It is said that he had found peace in the comfort of the Lord and then was buried right then and there by church members. Others say he spent the last of his days happy in the Mishpachah never to be seen by man again. The End!"

Noel sat, mouth open, staring at Boone. "That's your, I mean our church! Boone, the church in that story is our church! This is super cool!"

Boone was confused. "Yah, so, it's a story. How did you know that?"

"Well, I might have done some research online before you got here. And, I took notes during the assembly, see?" she bragged holding up a notebook with a few random scribbles on it.

"What! You made me tell that story and you already knew about it?" he asked.

She grinned and stated in her granny-voice, "Not all of it. I couldn't wait for you, and besides you did such a good job." Noel gathered some of the old books that surrounded her and pushed them towards Boone. "Start looking."

"For what?" he asked confused.

"I'm not sure," she said pulling together her own stack of books. "I was asking mom if she knew anything about the Craig guy or this Mish thing and she suggested I come up here and look."

"So what am I looking for exactly?"

"Like I said, I'm not real sure. When I researched the town and Mishpachah together, I got a lot of strange stuff. Like, did you know there is actually a society of people that meet once a year to discuss it's possible location!" She stopped to see if Boone was picking up on what she was implying.

"Are you trying to tell me that you want to find the Mishpachah?" he asked starting to laugh.

"I'm serious, Boone. This could be fun," she said putting down the book that she was holding and looking up at him. "Why not? It would be an adventure."

"But it's a story, something parents tell their kids so they won't ask for a bunch of stuff."

28

"Boone, please. I know that somewhere inside there is a piece of you that wants to know, a piece that wants the Mishpachah to be real. Didn't you ever want to set out looking for it when you were a kid?"

He had to admit that part of the idea did make him feel like a kid again. The other part terrified him, the part where he found himself in a quiet room talking to a deceased Elijah Craig. A few months ago he would not have hesitated and jumped right into this challenge feet first. Boone realized he had no choice, but to say 'yes'. If he said 'no' she would start asking more questions, and he didn't want her to think something was wrong with him. "I don't have anything else better to do. Where do we start?"

"See if you can find anything in these books, anything about the town history or Elijah Craig."

Boone shuffled through the books, blowing one hundred year old dust off the covers. "Where did you get these?"

"They were here when we moved in. That old lady at church, the one that gave us the house, must have left them here," Noel said, already lost in the literature. Boone sifted through title after title. He opened a few and then tossed them aside. He got up to stretch his legs and grab a new stack. His hand brushed something smooth and soft, unlike the gritty cloth covers of the piles before. Boone lifted the book to the top of his heap, sat back down, and ran his fingers across a symbol deeply embossed in its red leather. He swallowed hard and tried to ignore the nausea that was creeping into the pit of his stomach. There, pressed into the cover, was the image of the beehive. Reluctantly, Boone turned back the cover and read: *A True Record of the Great Crossing,* and then shut it quickly not wanting to read any further. His heart raced, but he couldn't tear his eyes away, feeling forced to look upon the imprint.

"What did you find?" Noel asked looking up from her mound of writings. Boone thrust the book at her with a feeling that he had found what she was looking for. "It's beautiful!" she exclaimed as she allowed her fingertips to rub over the design as Boone had done.

"I've seen it before," he mumbled.

"The book?" she questioned.

"No…the beehive."

"Sure, it's a beehive."

Boone leaned over to her. "See the circle?" he instructed touching the book. "See how the beehive is inside the ring? That same symbol is on one of the windows at church. It kind of caught my attention last Sunday." The attic room had grown darker as nighttime approached, even with the glow of the single light bulb dangling in the middle of the room. The draft that came with the early fall rain made its way effortlessly through the boarded walls. Boone shivered.

Noel opened the book and turned the pages gently as if they were a fine china or ancient artifact. Her eyes jumped to meet Boone's. "The church has a library?"

"We don't, as far as I know." Boone peeked over Noel's shoulder and read out loud the page that had first caught his attention, "*A True History of the Great Crossing* by Samuel Covington." He saw again the symbol that graced the cover of the book and adorned the church window and read on, "From the Library of Great Crossing Baptist Church, 1898."

"Boone, this is amazing!" Noel beamed with delight.

The uneasiness continued to churn inside of him. "So maybe they tore the library down when the new building was built."

"What do you mean *new* building?"

"All I know is mom and dad said homecoming was for 85 years in the *new* building. Since Craig was one of the pastors, the church itself is older than the building." He was proud of himself for the conclusion he had come to.

Noel turned another page and read, "Volume Seven of Forty. Table of Contents. Chapter One. Elijah Craig: Pioneer and Preacher." She diligently thumbed a few pages in the book and handed it to Boone. "Here, you read it."

He didn't argue. An unexplainable eagerness had started to replace his belly full of butterflies. Boone swallowed hard again and read, "The Reverend Elijah Craig began his life in Orange County, Virginia. The son of Toliver Craig... He was the 5th child..."

"Skip ahead, that's blah, blah, blah about his life," Noel recommended. "Find the section about your...err...I mean *our* church." To Boone, there wasn't a bad thing about Noel, but it really irritated him how often she implied the significant differences in their places of worship.

"Okay," he said glancing over the pages and mumbling as he went. "Established first classical school, set up grain mill, limestone water of Royal Springs to develop... preached at several churches...here it is! The Reverend Elijah Craig became the pastor of The Great Crossing Baptist Church and...." His narration trailed off.

"And what?" Noel almost shouted jumping to her feet.

"And nothing."

"What do you mean nothing?"

"I mean there is nothing about his time at the church, his wealth, or his death anywhere! A page has been torn out," Boone answered innocently, feeling the now frigid air pricking his skin. Noel anxiously reached for the book, not as delicately as she had handled it the first time, and rummaged through the remaining pages.

Boone shivered and hugged himself to keep warm. "Boone, are you all right?"

"It's freezing!"

Noel reached up and placed the palm of her hand on Boone's forehead. "Boone, it has to be at least eighty degrees up here. It's not even kind of cold."

"I don't know. Maybe I'm coming down with something."

"MOOOOOOOMMMMM! They're up here!" the thinning scream of Kaylee trailed up the narrow attic stair casing.

"Boone, don't tell anyone about this. Call the guys. We'll meet tomorrow after school," Noel said anxiously.

"Noel," Boone shivered, "why the guys?"

"Just do it Boone! We'll need their help. I have an idea."

Boone turned to walk away, but then he heard it, *"To him that worketh not."*

He shot a look back at Noel. "What did you say?"

"Huh?" Noel mumbled immersed in the red leather library book.

"Never mind," he sighed turning again to walk away.

"To him that worketh not." The words crept stealthily into his mind. He stopped and inhaled the scent of old house, damp lumber, rusty nails, and dust-carpeted floors. *"You are him!"* Boone deliberated a minute and then decided for now to ignore the voice that had chosen to haunt him.

Chapter 4

Noel waited impatiently under the red awning of Fava's, the town's oldest restaurant, with a stack of books in her arms and backpack slung over her shoulder. She had taken the bus home that afternoon as she often did and then walked from her house to the downtown establishment. Today the boys had decided the walk from school would be more fun. "Boys, let's get to work," she said opening the wood framed glass door releasing the aroma of warm hamburgers and newly fried French fries.

"I say we eat first. Then you can tell us about all the madness you've got Boone wrapped up in," Wayne commented before racing to the corner booth by the window. Fava's had been around long before any of them, the boys had grown up with it. Case swore that he had eaten his 100th bacon cheeseburger by the time he was nine. Boone had heard Noel talk about a similar ice cream parlor in her hometown, so it was easy to convince her that this should be their meeting place.

The red walls of the long rectangular room echoed the interests of not only the new owners, but also those who took comfort in the company of other locals. University of Kentucky memorabilia hung comfortably alongside antique knick-knacks. Behind the cash register, floor-to-ceiling shelving displayed a compilation of Mickey Mouse treasures that had been acquired and donated over the years.

"Case, what are you doing here?" a slender redheaded girl asked sarcastically.

"Eating," Case replied flatly. "Nice apron, sis!"

The older female parallel of Case rolled her eyes. "Let me guess, the usual: two bacon cheeseburgers no onions, one with no mayo, one Giant Fava burger, three Fava chips, two orders fried banana peppers, three full size chocolate milkshakes, and for dessert one coconut, one butterscotch, and one chocolate pie. How did I do?"

"Nice," Boone approved. "How about you Noel?"

"Seriously, you guys are pigs," she laughed scanning the menu for new additions before placing her order. "I'll have a patty melt, no onions please, curly seasoned fries, water with no ice, and a hot fudge cake for dessert."

"Got it! I'll get it out to you as soon as I can, and Case, don't come back there asking what's taking so long. You're gonna get me fired," she huffed walking away from the group. Ten short minutes later, the young waitress returned with an assortment of plates stretching arm to arm. Another waitress steadied a tray a few feet behind her carrying the hodgepodge of milkshakes and desserts. "Please tell me that's it?"

"For now," Case said, diving face first into his food.

"Okay, has Boone explained why you are here?" The excitement in Noel's voice was clear.

"Nope," Wayne answered with his mouth full of burger.

Noel gave Boone an irritated glare. "Last night, Boone and I found this," she said as she pulled the red leather book from her backpack. Its appearance was like a lantern on a dreary day. Boone couldn't help but feel that the golden beehive was shining intentionally for him. "It's about Elijah Craig."

Wayne looked up from his plate of half eaten banana peppers. "You mean the dead guy from school the other day? Who cares about him?"

"Boone does," Noel announced casually sipping her water. "Right, Boone?"

Boone choked on the piece of burger he was trying to swallow. He knew he was stuck and he knew what was coming next. She was about to tell them about the Mishpachah. It would be more ammo for Case and Wayne to pester her, and if they knew he was really in to it, he would never live it down. "Um…sure," he said insensitively shoving another wad of fries in his mouth.

"Wayne," she continued seriously, "that dead guy used to be a pastor at your church." She corrected herself before one of the guys had the chance to, "I mean *our* church."

"So," Wayne and Case said in unison.

Noel took a bite of her patty melt and a couple of fries and swallowed. She opened the book and read, "The Reverend Elijah Craig became the pastor of The Great Crossing Baptist Church and…".

"And what?" Case asked exposing his minute curiosity.

"It doesn't say," Boone said taking over for a moment. "The next page is missing. That's all we know."

"Actually," Noel interrupted, "that's not all. I did some research online and found that there are people who really believe that Elijah Craig's Mishpachah exists! There are lots of people who believe he really found it, and even more who are looking for it today. Many of these people believe the entrance is somewhere on the church property. So, we need to find his grave, or at least where it is supposed to be and then we will have our first clue to finding the Mishpachah!"

Wayne and Case stared at her dumbfounded. "Great, well at least we got a good meal out of it," Wayne reasoned swallowing his last bite of his butterscotch pie. "Pinks, you are hilarious!"

"It's not a joke," she begged. "Boone, tell them!"

He was trapped between something that had haunted him for days and two friends that had been with him since diapers. Her eyes pleaded for support.

"Guys, wait." Boone knew there had to be more. "There's more, right Noel?"

"Of course," she stammered. The crack in her voice gave away that her feelings had been hurt, and Boone was sure that his hesitation had contributed. "At the end of the chapter on Mr. Craig it states, 'the fellowship of the Great Crossing Baptist Church will be forever grateful for the generous offering entrusted to us by the Reverend Elijah Craig." She put the book in her backpack and started to stand, leaving her uneaten fudge cake on the table. Boone knew something was wrong. She never let anything chocolate go uneaten. "It's proof that at least part of his story is true. Why would someone tear a page from a book if they weren't trying to hide something…" She waited for them to respond, but they didn't. "Like the location of the Mishpachah!"

"Sorry Noel, not buyin' it," Case admitted. "It's a story." She looked to Boone for support. How could he even begin to convince the guys of everything that had happened to him so far? He knew now that they would never believe him.

"I thought I could count on you Boone," she said before walking over to the cash register to pay for her half eaten meal.

"Noel, I didn't mean to hurt your feelings," he tried to explain as he rushed over to her. "Don't go. Sit back down."

"Boone, you made me look stupid over there. I don't know if any of this is real, but last night you were excited to find the Mishpachah! So what if it's a child's story. You let me down, Boone," she snapped, looking up at him with a glisten of tears in her eyes, before turning to walk out the door.

Again, Boone found himself not knowing what to say. He was never very good at dealing with emotions. In fact, he couldn't even remember the last time he had cried. "She's a girl, she'll get over it," Wayne reassured, patting him on the shoulder and stepping up to pay. "The sun's coming out. Let's go back to our house and play ball." Boone didn't feel much like basketball that day, especially since Wayne was good enough to be on the basketball team, and Boone knew he would be easily beaten. But, he agreed hoping that hanging out with the guys would make the uncomfortable feeling inside of him go away.

Just then, the bell on the door clanged. Boone, Case, and Wayne gulped as Elijah Craig stepped through the door. This time, he was dressed in blue jeans and a Georgetown College sweatshirt. "Hey, Bev, can I get a burger and shake to go?" the man asked an elderly lady at the counter. "Hey kid, is the pie good today?"

"Excuse me?" Boone asked faintly.

"The pie, is it good today?" the actor repeated.

"It's always good," Boone answered awkwardly. He was shocked by the sudden appearance of the image of a man who minutes before had ruined his friendship. Wayne and Case left their change on the table and ran out the door. Boone remained behind, entranced by the actor who had portrayed the Reverend so effectively a few days before. He knew for once what it was he had to do.

T he next evening the shadow of the steeple blocked the sun from Boone's eyes. He sat in the circle of youth on the church lawn and stared angrily at the stained glass windows on the side of the brick church. The fall day was unusually warm, thus the reason why Reed had decided that Wednesday night youth group would be held outside. Boone scanned the group looking for Noel. They hadn't spoken a word since the day before at Fava's. She wouldn't even look at him at lunch. In fact she had sat quietly working on her homework while she ate, completely ignoring that he was sitting across from her. Boone had tried to catch her looking up so he could give her a smile, but she never gave him the chance. He knew that he had hurt her feelings and had even tried to apologize, but Noel had stormed out of Fava's Restaurant without looking back.

"Hey B!" Reed acknowledged checking out the group for an open spot in the circle. "Where's N?" He occasionally called the youth by their first initials. It annoyed everyone including Boone, but somehow they each had picked up the habit.

"Don't know," he said shrugging his shoulders. Noel was always there. If they gave an award for perfect attendance in Wednesday night youth group, Noel would have it. So, her absence was noticed.

"They're fighting," Case mumbled, lying down in the grass with his eyes closed. Boone heard a snicker from a body resting beside Case.

Jeff Morgan sat up, leaned back on his arms, and sneered at Boone. "The dynamic duo is fighting?" he asked coolly.

Boone jumped to his feet and stared directly into the calm eyes of Jeff. "It's none of your business, Jeff!" Jeff was on his feet before Boone could process what was happening.

"Are we seriously going to have a fight at church? I am SO glad I came!" Wayne shouted, which drew everyone's attention to the two boys. Boone had never felt so angry and so embarrassed at the same time. He hadn't been in a real fight before. He didn't think that a few arguments with his sister over stupid stuff like whose night it was to do the dishes even qualified as a fight.

As if awakened by the intensity of the moment, the voice returned to Boone. "*You are him*," it whispered, soothing his rage, blocking the comments of the teens, and allowing him to hear Reed's frantic words.

"All right guys, sit back," Reed urged in a clearly shaken voice. It was obvious to Boone and probably everyone else that this was Reed's first attempt at breaking up a fight.

Boone turned his back on Jeff and walked back to sit on the grass by Doug, a really short sixth grader who wore his winter coat year round. His heart still raced, but the anger had disappeared. He was worried about Noel. Surely he hadn't hurt her enough to keep her from church. She was stronger than that.

"Let's open with a short scripture and then I have a game," Reed sighed with apparent relief that the fight had not taken a turn for the physical. Boone had a Bible at home. It was nice, leather-bound and even had his name on it, but he rarely brought it. Doug jabbed him with his elbow and pushed his worn and tattered Bible in front of Boone, demonstrating his willingness to share. Boone took the offer and listened as Reed read. "For the body is not one member but many. If the foot says, 'because I am not a hand, I am not part of the body', it is not for this reason any the less a part of the body . . . "

Boone closed his eyes and allowed the warm evening to quietly woo his eyes to close. He quickly forced them back open. Reed was still reading. "But now God has placed the members, each one of them, in the body, just as He desired..." His eyes drifted shut again.

Shaking his head to knock off the weariness, he found himself no longer on the church lawn. Instead, he was alone inside the church sanctuary. The light that had shown on him last Sunday returned and drew his eye to the stained glass windows. The symbols were brighter, glowing vividly. The window inset with the beehive beamed clearer than the others, shining like the North Star, guiding him to an undisclosed location. He drifted towards to it. The closer he drew; the brighter it became. He climbed the stairs to touch it before the light went out. He was almost there. Its beauty sang to him and begged him to understand its calling.

Boone fearfully reached his hand to touch the beehive, afraid that a swarm would attack him if he disturbed their home. His finger connected with the cold glass. At first, there was an insignificant pop. It was instantly followed by a trickle of similar sounds that produced a skinny crack on the hand painted image beneath his finger. The fracture expanded quickly, branching off into thinner lines until thousands of lines danced in front of him. With a violent crash, the glass smashed to the floor and fell into heaps of tiny shards at his feet. He reluctantly glanced down at the room below. Tear stained faces looked back at him. He tried to speak, to explain that it wasn't his fault, but his mouth wouldn't open. Their eyes stayed fixed on him. Boone wanted to run, but the only way out of the church was down through the weeping congregation below. Beams of light were shining through on all sides of the church. What was happening to him? He was going to be sick. He had to get out! He ran down the stairs as windows crashed to the ground one-by-one behind him. "You are him! What do we do, Boone? Tell us Boone! What do we do?" they shouted. Their voices grew louder and more unified.

"Boone? Boone?" Boone awoke to the frustrated voice of Reed. He couldn't help but look back to the church windows. They were still there, lined up on the brick walls, and prepared to capture the evening sun. The queasiness returned. He couldn't make it stop. He jumped to his feet and ran to the far side of the parking lot. Boone fell to his knees and threw up. For now, he didn't care if he ever had another burger at Fava's again.

He could hear the muffled voices of the group's girls whispering words like *gross* and *disgusting* to one another. He stumbled a few feet from where he had allowed himself to be sick and sat down on the cold pavement. With his back to the group, he breathed in the freshness of the farmland in front of him.

Boone knew that he had a few minutes alone before Reed would send someone to check on him. "I'm going crazy," he thought, "I, Boone Tackett, am insane!"

Jeff was reading loud enough for Boone to hear. "And if one member suffers, all the members suffer with it."

Boone smirked, "I am definitely suffering alone on this one." He looked over the acres of rolling green farmland and then to the modest family graveyard on the far right edge of the church property. He, Wayne, and Case used to play in there secretly as kids, but it had kind of lost its allure as they had gotten older. Two very weathered obelisk shaped tombstones jutted over the top of the limestone wall. One of which, by way of its missing top, revealed evidence of a lost battle with the elements. In the back corner, a tree loomed over the exterior wall.

For the first time, Boone allowed his logic to think about the dead man that was possibly buried there. He wondered if that was the tree of legend he had heard about his entire life. Why had he never permitted his imagination to connect his childhood bedtime story to the one tree on the church property? A tree whose roots ran firmly under a graveyard? A ginger colored leaf from the tree wriggled free from its home on the branch. Boone watched it fall, wondering if it would land perfectly on one of the headstones; but instead, it fell perfectly on a real head. "Noel?" he called louder than he had intended. Several of the youth shot a look back at him. Boone clutched his waist and faked a loud moan. Effectively grossed out, they instantly looked away not wanting to witness the dismissal of the rest of Boone's school lunch.

"You all right Boone?" Reed called to him by name, dropping the use of his first initial to show sincerity.

Boone nodded and gave a halfhearted wave. Reed graced him with a concerned look and then refocused on the group. Boone knew his mom would be receiving a call from him tonight.

He waited for Noel to appear again. Realizing now that no one was coming anywhere close to him, he crawled toward the cemetery and sat with his back to the wall, keeping his head down. "What are you doing?" he mumbled under a covered mouth so no one could see that he was talking.

"I'm not talking to you," she argued.

"I said I was sorry!"

"So, leave me alone. This has nothing to do with you anymore."

Boone checked to see if anyone was looking his way. "I saw the tree. It has to be the same one." Noel didn't respond. "Are you okay?"

"I don't know," she said starting to cry. Boone didn't know how to relate to this side of her, but he did know he didn't want her to be upset. "I thought this might be something fun, but you didn't say anything when they laughed at me. You always let them laugh at me. Why do you do that Boone?" He started to answer, but she kept going. "So what if I *accidentally* dyed my hair pink? So what if I like an adventure every now and then? So do you! Remember? It doesn't matter anymore anyway. This whole thing is stupid. And you know what, Elijah Craig, if he's in here at all, is probably buried under the parking lot beside his mom! There isn't even a headstone for him in here, unless his real name was Nancy, and I doubt that…"

"Well," Boone tried to change the subject, "isn't that kind of strange that there isn't a tombstone for him. The church said they would be forever grateful. Seems like they would have left him with more than asphalt, don't you think? Hey, have you been in here this whole time looking for a grave?"

"I guess," Noel sniffled.

"Listen, I think we should have a look at the windows in the church," Boone suggested.

"Why?" He checked again to see what the group was doing. It looked like charades because Doug was flapping his arms up and down while the others reclined awkwardly on the grass, but he couldn't be sure. "Let's say it's a gut feeling. At least check out the beehive window. We will call it a clue." He was actually scared of looking at it. He was afraid that it would shatter like in his dream.

"Okay," she answered, finally standing to her feet. "We can do it Saturday after flashlight tag." She stopped talking to think. "Boone, Jeff asked me to be his partner. I told him 'yes'."

"What!" Boone jumped to his feet not caring who was watching. "Why him? You and I, we're always partners!"

"I'm mad at you." She stood up with her hands covered in dirt and her clothes muddy. "He asked me on Sunday. So I told him at school today that I would. He's nice to me. You ought to try and like him - I don't know why you don't."

"Whatever," Boone mumbled. "Saturday night plan to stay after, okay? I'll have mom take you home." He started to walk away and then turned back to see Noel holding the dead leaf in her hand. "Noel, I think you may be on to something." He wanted to tell her more, tell her everything, but he knew this wasn't the time or the place. Boone fixated curiously on the tree. He smiled reassuringly at Noel, and then ventured away past the church and towards home.

Chapter 5

Over the past month, Boone had allowed his dirty clothes to bury not only his bed and dresser, but also a pile of deserted camping equipment from summer vacation. Copies of his favorite outdoor magazine and graded homework from the start of the school year had made its way under the bed, nightstand, and into his closet. But now, all was in order, at least until the disaster crept back into his room and prompted his mother's raised eyebrows. The room wasn't big, but had taken him more than an hour to clean. Boone plopped down on his freshly made bed, wrinkling the quilted blanket beneath him. He gazed up at the glow-in-the-dark stars that had been on his ceiling since he was in the fourth grade. "Why take them down now?" he thought.

His bed was a giant sponge that soaked in every bit of his exhaustion. It had been a long day for Boone. He had been in a fight with Noel, tried to make up with her, almost gotten himself in a fight with Jeff for a reason he couldn't even remember, was having nightmares during the day, and had puked during the middle of youth group. He couldn't imagine that his life could get anymore uncomfortable, until he remembered that he still had homework.

The navy blue three-ring binder that held his English assignment stared at him from the corner of his desk. The revision of his personal narrative wasn't due until Friday. He figured he had one more day to work on it. Boone contemplated its completion and the relief he would feel of having Ms. Shelly's assignment over and done with. He placed his hands over his eyes to think, merely to see the shattering of a church window and millions of tiny colored pieces falling like confetti to the ground.

Boone sat up on the edge of his bed. "English can definitely wait," he decided. He moved over to his desk and turned on the desktop computer. The machine grunted and groaned. He tapped his fingers as he impatiently waited for his archaic device to start up. It was nearing bedtime and he had a lot to find out.

He abandoned his computer and jerked open the drawer of his nightstand. He grabbed his leather bound Bible, a journal given to him by his grandfather on his 12th birthday, and a flashlight, jammed them into his backpack, and ran out of his room and past the kitchen to the front door where a series of hooks hung organizing the Tackett's family key collection. Boone grabbed the set marked GCBC. "Going to use the Internet at church!" he yelled back to his mom who was busy making oatmeal chocolate chip cookies with his sister.

"Did you clean your room?"

"Yes!" he answered.

"Be home by 9:30, Boone. No later!" Mrs. Tackett reminded him, "It's a school night!"

"Yes, Mom!" Boone started out the door once again.

"Son," his dad called, "don't forget to lock the church."

"K!" Boone hollered back, finally making his way out the door and across the street to the church. He sprinted through the darkness of the empty parking lot to a set of narrow concrete steps that led up to the side entrance of the sanctuary. His hand clutched the wrought iron railing to steady himself. From the top of the steps he could see the tombstones in the graveyard. Boone chuckled at the thought of Noel crawling around in there during youth group earlier that evening. Then he remembered her anger and how she had agreed to be Jeff's flashlight tag partner. With a sigh, he put that thought aside realizing that he had two more days until he really had to worry about that. The wooden door creaked as he slowly pushed it open. He turned around and shut it behind him with a *thud* that echoed in the still room.

The light of the full moon shined through the stained glass windows on the far side of the sanctuary, creating an eerie glow throughout the room of worship. Immediately, his eyes were drawn to the painted glass image of the open Bible and the words "to him that worketh not." Memories of the past few days came flooding back to him so fast that he shut his eyes ready for the windows to shatter or the chandelier to start flashing on and off. He opened them slowly with relief. Thankfully, there was nothing except the *tick, tick* of the clock behind him. "Time to get some answers," Boone said aloud as he navigated through the sanctuary and down an unlit hallway to the church office where his mother had volunteered since he was a baby.

The tiny space had enough room for two desks and a bookshelf. Boone's seventh grade school picture was framed and displayed proudly by his sister's on the closer of the two. He flopped down into the swiveling office chair, signed onto the computer with his mom's password, and clicked the icon designated for the Internet. The Internet at the church was twice as fast as what he had at home; and since Boone's mom was also the church secretary, she often let him use her laptop. Immediately, his connection to the world was in front of him. He typed in the words 'to him that worketh not' in the empty box at the top left of the screen.

A list of possibilities appeared in front of him. Not knowing which to choose from, Boone moved his mouse to the first one and opened a black page with an open Bible at the top. "But to him that worketh not," he read distinctly, "but believeth on Him that justifieth the ungodly, his faith is counted for righteousness. Romans 4:5." He read it again and again, searching for some clue as to what was happening to him. "Work and faith," he reread. "What's that have to do with me? I cleaned my room today, that was a lot of work!"

Methodically, he began to mentally shuffle through the visions, dreams and bizarre encounters. Boone thought about the bees and his disaster in science class on Monday. They were working so hard and so fast, as if stopping would discontinue their existence. He had an idea. "Work! The beehive!"

His fingers moved quickly across the keyboard, anxiously typing in the words "beehive" and "worketh." His eyes examined the suggested web addresses until they connected with the phrase 'Old Testament'. "The first part of the Bible," Boone said curiously. He slid the digital arrow over the link and clicked. The text flew across the screen unveiling multiple Biblical references to *honey*. Over and over, he saw the phrase, 'land flowing with milk and honey' repeated throughout various scriptures. "The beehive is often used as a symbol for a plentiful and prosperous land," he read. "Honey itself appears in the account of Sampson in which he took it from the corpse of a lion. The Bible also states in the book of Psalms that the law and judgments of the Lord are sweeter than honey."

Boone's heart beat rapidly and his thoughts wondered out of control; he couldn't help but think that the prosperous land might be the Mishpachah. He grabbed his backpack, shut the computer, and ran back to the sanctuary. The moonlight had diminished behind October clouds leaving Boone in complete darkness. He reached for his flashlight and used it to inspect each of the church's windows. Stained glass birds, crosses, boats and tablets were brought to life by the flashlight's beam. He took a second to sketch each one inside of his journal and record any information from the windows individual nameplates. The rectangular plates said things like 'presented to' and 'in memory of', dedications to members of the church that were now long gone.

Boone looked at his watch. He had a little bit longer until curfew. He dashed up the left side staircase toward the balcony to document the details of the upstairs windows. Alone in the dark corridor, he had a sudden feeling of déjà vu. He was standing exactly where he had been in his dream earlier that day, in front of the beehive.

Boone apprehensively surveyed the room and then cautiously reached up to touch the image. He closed his eyes in expectation of the worst. With hesitation, but out of curiosity, he peered over the railing to look for the mysterious congregation he had seen in his dream. He was still alone. Boone, with his back against the ornate handrail, slid down to sit on the crimson-carpeted floor.

"Are you kidding?" he loudly asked the empty room. "Are you kidding? What am I doing?" He realized that all this time he had hoped that there was some sort of meaning behind what was happening to him, but all he had was a journal full of sketches and phrases. "It's just a myth! The Mishpachah isn't real! Who in their right mind could think a place like that could exist! Apparently, I do, or I wouldn't be sitting here in the dark! I'm out of here," he yelled. "Did you hear that Elijah Craig? I'm done. So, leave me alone and let me get back to my life!"

Boone stood up swiftly and turned to grab his backpack. In doing so, he noticed that the nameplate below the beehive held no words of condolence or devotion. It was clearly blank. "That's strange," he mumbled. Bright lights from outside panned the room. Someone had pulled into the parking lot. He knew it wasn't his parents; they never drove to the church unless it was raining really hard. He crouched back down on the balcony floor to peer between the metal railings. A key lightly jingled at the side door. Boone squinted to see the doorknob turning. He couldn't imagine why anyone would be at the church this late on a Wednesday night. He definitely didn't feel like explaining why he was up in the balcony when he was supposed to be on the computer downstairs. He sprinted to the back of the loft, swerved to avoid bumping into one of the pews, and ducked into the slightly open door of an upstairs classroom. Just then, the white wooden side door swung open.

Boone tried to quiet his breathing. Timidly, he stuck his head out of the room to get a better look. Boone couldn't make out who it was. He wanted to get closer, but he knew there was nowhere to go without being seen. He waited impatiently for the body to walk into the light provided by the headlights of the vehicle parked outside. As the image became clearer, he could distinguish the figure of a male teen standing by the antiquated organ. Boone watched his hand grab something dainty and shiny from its top. Then, the person vanished, but the door to the church was still open. Boone looked around frantically. Footsteps echoed one by one on the staircase opposite him. Boone retreated into the classroom, tripping over an open box and bumping his head on what he concluded was a table leg. "Ouch!" he gasped.

"You all right?" Jeff said looking down over him and extending his hand to offer help. Boone noticed that Jeff strangely kept his other hand behind his back. Whatever he had taken from the piano, he didn't want Boone to see it.

Boone took the available hand. "I think so. What are you doing here?"

"Picking up something for my grandmother."

Jeff pulled Boone to his feet and asked, "And you?"

"And me what?" Boone asked back.

"What are you doing here?"

Boone thought quickly, "I was, um, looking for my Bible. I think I left it here." He pretended to look around the unofficial storage area that at one time had been a classroom.

"Right," Jeff replied doubtfully as he turned his back and withdrew from the room.

"Hey Jeff?" Boone asked curiously. Jeff stopped and turned back around. "How did you know I was up here?"

"You left your flashlight on Boone," Jeff informed him. "You might want to save those batteries for Saturday night."

He started to walk back towards the stairs. Then he stopped to look at Boone who was still standing in the doorway of the classroom. "I hope you're not mad that I'm borrowing your friend for an evening," Jeff commented before walking away.

In that moment, Boone could not think of one witty response. The heat of anger was rising in his face; he could feel it. The anger that had been inside him earlier that day was pushing its way back to the surface, and to add to that, it was already 9:30 and he knew he would be in trouble. With flashlight in hand, Boone went back into the room to get his stuff. His light dimly lit up the cluttered area, and to his surprise, more windows. He had forgotten that there were windows tucked into each of the sanctuary's eight classrooms. The revelation worked its magic in soothing his rage and reengaging his excitement. "Three more, I'll copy three more, and then I'll go home," he mouthed as he removed his journal from his backpack. The anticipation of some left behind secret drew him back in like an addiction.

Two of the windows were unobstructed and easily observable. A third was barely visible. Boone climbed over boxes of old hymnals and pushed aside piles of maps to get to it. He lifted his flashlight to the window and shouted, "AHHH!" as he stumbled backward over a basket of artificial flowers. There, represented in stained glass, was a snake, mouth open and fangs extended, wrapped tightly around a cross. Boone quickly tried to reproduce the image in his journal. There was creepiness to this particular one, something dark and mysterious that separated it from the others. He shuddered, nearly dropping his pencil among the forgotten clutter.

Boone cautiously flicked the light around the room one last time. In front of him a pale yellow rectangular glass panel rested on a window ledge. He picked it up and read:

In Appreciation of the Sacrificial
Faith of "The Founders" & Loyal Members of this Church
The Fidelis Matron's Class

Boone carefully set it down and studied the spot from where it had been removed. The symbol above it was that of a hand pointing down from a giant cloud, as if acknowledging where the pane should have been. The empty space below the window had no sign of breakage or damage. The panel had simply been removed. *Who would take this off?* he contemplated. *Better yet, why did they take it off?*

His watch read 9:45. *Gotta go! The others have to wait,* he thought. He shoved the book back in his pack, zipped the top, and then flung it over his shoulder. Still baffled at the broken window, Boone left the classroom and ran down the stairs. Remembering his father's last words, 'Don't forget to lock the church back,' he reached in his jeans pocket for the keys. A blinding light flashed in his eyes. He blocked its intensity with the palm of his hand, but was able to catch a glimpse of a large black SUV with Jeff in the passenger seat pulling away from the church. *They were waiting on me to leave,* Boone thought. He decided to wave and smile innocently to avoid suspicion.

The issues in his life were certainly stacking up. As with the others, he decided that dealing with this one would have to wait until later. Right now, there was one thing that he could think about. It was the one thing that he believed would make everything return to normal - finding the Mishpachah.

Chapter 6

Boone moved further into the darkness to get a better look at the manifestation in front of him. He crept closer, being careful not to anger it into repositioning its beast like hands into him. The distorted figure's head hung low. Its shoulders hunched over as if carrying a load far heavier than it could bear on its own. If Boone hadn't been so afraid, he would have been certain that the creature in some way needed him. In its one hand, a creamy gold substance dripped to the nothingness below. In the other, it clutched a book so tightly that its long, brittle and jagged fingernails dug deep into the symbol inscribed on the supple red leather. Boone recognized instantly its similarity to the one he and Noel had found a couple days earlier in her attic.

The creature raised its head sadly, revealing weary and yellowed eyes. Boone stumbled backwards, aware that the freakish being before him was a horrifying deformation of himself. In a voice of exhaustion and fear, it spoke. "It's not about you. Find the Mishpachah and beware of the wolves." The creature turned away despairingly and disappeared into the black.

Boone was completely alone. He tried to move, but his feet would not allow him to go where his eyes could not see to plant them. "Help! Anyone! Help me!" he screamed, but not even he could hear his own words. He desperately longed to have the company of another life, even if that other life was the grotesquely altered version of his self. The loneliness burned at his throat and caused him to thirst for a drink denied by the absence of time. In the cavernous vacuum of unreality, days, weeks, and years melted into a timeless soup.

His mind filled with hopelessness in his isolation from the world. He was frantic to find a way out of this nightmare, a way out of his own dream world. Hot salty tears burned in streams down his cheeks as sorrow enveloped his soul.

Beep, beep, beep. It was the distant sound of his alarm clock that finally woke him from his distressed state. He groggily realized it was Saturday morning and that only the night had passed over him. Boone drifted through his morning routine surreally unable to shake the feeling of loneliness the night terror had presented to him. Even now as he sat on the porch watching Case and Wayne strolling across the lawn towards him, he couldn't ignore the feeling that the dream was real. Over the past few days, he had come to expect the dreams with sleep, but this one beat them all. The emotions that the nightmare had left him with were very real, and from that he could not awake.

The past few days had come and gone slowly for Boone. His mom hadn't been kidding when she had told him to be home by 9:30 a few nights before. So now, he ultimately found himself at the end of a two-day, no phone, no friends grounding. Sitting on his front porch dressed in the usual worn out blue jeans and faded t-shirt, Boone checked his backpack for the fifth time to make sure he had everything he might need. He went through his mental checklist: a flashlight for flashlight tag, his journal containing the notes and drawings he had done of the windows, his Bible and a few random camping items he had stuffed into his closet. While he patiently waited for Case and Wayne to near his house, he recalled the sequence of last night's nightmare, and the unquenchable thirst for answers to the questions he still had.

He gathered his things and proceeded to join them. The three of them crossed the street and walked into the church parking lot as they had done many times before. A few of the youth were already standing on the church's front steps with flashlights in hand. Parent-driven cars circled into the lot to drop off more eager and excited teens. Boone watched as the same black SUV from that eventful night a few days ago pulled under the carport to the side of the church. The passenger door flung open. Jeff leaped from the car toting two flashlights, and jogged over towards the group.

"He's a little too excited for flashlight tag don't ya think?" Wayne asked sarcastically as he leaned into Boone. Boone laughed out loud to make sure everyone heard him, including Jeff.

"Hey guys," Jeff greeted.

"Hey!" Noel gleefully acknowledged. Her jolly presence caught Boone so off balance that he fell over sideways into Wayne.

"Hey…" Boone answered back pulling himself off of his friend. He shouldn't have been surprised that she was speaking to Jeff so casually. Jeff started to say something to her, but Boone interrupted, he couldn't wait any longer to share with Noel what he had found. "I need to talk to you Noel. It's important." He lightly tugged at her arm to pull her aside.

Jeff stepped up to them, "Noel, is everything okay?"

"She's fine," Boone answered for her.

Noel glared at Boone, and then smiled at Jeff. "I'm fine, give me a sec, okay?"

Boone waited for Jeff to walk away before speaking. "I have to show you something."

"Don't be rude Boone. I have a partner and I'm not going to be tricked into playing with you!"

"Noel," he looked sternly at her, "it's the Mishpachah. You were right! People have been *here* looking for it."

"What?"

"I know I haven't exactly been myself lately, but I found something upstairs. Please let me show you."

"I don't know Boone, Jeff is waiting for me. I already told you I would stay later." She looked down at her feet. "Can I trust you?"

The question hit him hard. They were best friends; trust had never been an issue. "Of course," he insisted. The sound of hurt was apparent in his voice.

"Boone, I feel like you've been hiding things from me. Then there's the whole Fava's thing. I…"

He stopped her, knowing it was time to share what he had been holding back. "Noel, I think I'm going crazy. I'm seeing people and things that can't be real. I'm having nightmares all the time, and I don't think they will stop until I find the Mishpachah!"

She glanced at Jeff again. He was still looking their way. "Okay, give me a minute," Noel requested stepping in Jeff's general direction.

Noel looked back at Boone and then continued her talk with the preacher's son. Jeff leaned over and whispered something in her ear. Jealousy flared up in Boone at the sight of the two of them together. Frustrated, he crossed his arms, turned his head the other way and sulked into the church alone.

"Wait up!" Noel called to him. Boone's heart skipped as he turned to see her running towards him. "You have ten minutes and that's it!"

"Thanks! What did you tell him?"

"Nothing important. Ten minutes Boone, that's all you have!"

"Deal!" He grabbed her hand and pulled her into the church where the final stages of the setting sun cast gigantic shadows across the sanctuary.

"All right Boone, show me!" she said excitedly.

"Hear me out. The symbol on the book was a beehive, right?" Boone led her upstairs to the window that had invaded his dreams. He sat down on the floor, unzipped his backpack, pulled out his journal, and opened it to where he had scribbled and drawn a few nights before. Boone translated his scratchy handwriting, "*A beehive is often the symbol for a land flowing with milk and honey or a prosperous land.* I think this beehive is a clue to finding the Mishpachah? Maybe it's some lesser piece of a bigger puzzle that will lead us there!"

"Okay, I'm tracking with you, but didn't we kind of know the beehive was important?" Noel surveyed each of the symbols around the church as they rested within their stained glass homes. She then placed her hand on the empty nameplate. "That's odd. Why is this one the only one that's blank?"

"I thought the same thing the other night! Each window was presented by or in memory of someone a long time ago when the new building was constructed. So the question is, what makes this one so different?"

Noel appeared to be deep in thought, running her fingers back and forth over the plate. "What if it's not what's supposed to be on the plate, but what's behind it?"

"You read my mind! And that's what I really have to show you! Follow me!" The shadows in the open room had collected into nightfall. Boone flipped on his flashlight and led Noel through the heavy white door at the back of the balcony. He flicked his light around the room until it landed on the detached plate he had seen three nights earlier.

Noel gasped, "Boone! Did you do that?"

"No," Boone said surprised that she would even think he would. "Remember how I told you that someone else might be looking for the Mishpachah? Look at the hand above it; it's pointing down to the plate. I was thinking…"

"You were thinking again?" she giggled.

"Ha, ha, very funny. I was thinking that whoever removed this plate must have figured the same thing, that some clue to the Mishpachah would be behind it and that hand points to it."

"Maybe." Noel carefully picked up the upset plate and read the inscription. "Sacrificial faith…the founders. Boone, you're right. This didn't fall off on its own. But I don't think that whomever it was found what they were looking for. Look, the hand has two fingers pointing downward, almost more like they are reaching for something." She lifted her hand and pointed to Boone. "When someone is pointing to something they want you to see, they point with one finger, not two. Anyway, whoever did this sure thought they were looking in the right spot."

"But they weren't, and we know where to look!" Boone bragged.

"Boone Tackett, don't even think about it! We are not defacing church property!"

"Fine, then what do you suggest?"

"Well, actually…"

"Wait!" Boone froze. In the distance, he heard the chatter of conversation. "They can't find us up here. We can't tell anyone about this, not yet."

"I agree Boone. It has been ten minutes. I need to find Jeff."

"Alright," he surrendered. "I'll help you find him. He's probably headed to the basement with the others." The two tiptoed down the creaking stairs into the sanctuary and then immediately made a turn to go down a second flight of stairs into the basement below. Primarily used for baby showers and potluck dinners, the church basement was large and open. It stayed cool even in the hottest of summer days. Folding tables and chairs were scattered about in anticipation of the pizza dinner that was to end the evening's event. "That's strange. I would have sworn that I heard voices down here."

"Boone, let's go outside. They're probably still out there."

"But, I heard them." Boone stopped in the basement room to listen; his eyes searched the white cabinets in the kitchen area and metal piping that ran across the low ceiling. Again he heard a faint collection of voices. "Don't you hear that?"

"Hear what?" Noel asked eyeballing Boone suspiciously.

"The voices. I know I heard them down here. Didn't you hear them?" Hurriedly, Boone started pacing the room searching for the source of the ramblings. The sound grew louder as he neared the storeroom door. Out of the corner of his eye, he saw Noel suspiciously watching him. Boone reached for the doorknob and gave it a really quick turn. He yanked it open to reveal the church's heating and cooling unit, shelving stacked floor to ceiling with cleaning goods, and old Christmas decorations.

"What's with you Boone?" Noel questioned. "Voices, nightmares…you're kind of beginning to scare me."

"I don't know. I thought I heard people talking, whispering. It was so loud. But now, there's nothing." Anxiety covered his suntanned face.

"Maybe you should sit down," Noel motioned to an upturned bucket. Boone sat slowly, dropped his head, and placed his hands over his ears.

"Seriously, are you okay?"

Boone looked up to his friend who was now leaning against the doorframe. "I don't think so," he answered. Noel stepped toward him. As she did, the door slammed behind her leaving the two of them in the dark. She swiftly turned and reached back to grab the doorknob, but the door locked, trapping them inside. "Now what?"

"We wait until the group comes down. Then we can yell for someone to let us out," she suggested, crossing her legs and sitting on the floor. The two sat in silence thinking over all the mysterious discoveries they had made this week. He remembered his dream and the unappeasable thirst that he had been feeling all day. The pieces weren't coming together. He re-examined and tried to organize his thoughts, but all he felt was chaos and confusion.

"Water!" Noel blurted out. "Boone, you're not hearing voices! It's water!"

"What?" Boone questioned as Noel's voice interrupted his thinking.

"Don't you hear it?"

"Okay, this is not funny! I really did hear voices; and now, you're making fun of me?"

"Hush, Boone, and listen." She crawled to the back of the space, feverishly searching every inch of the room. She stopped to shove a box of paper towels and an industrial sized bottle of hand soap out of the way.

Boone did as she had asked. The soft sound of moving water drifted through his mind. He lunged to her side, took out his flashlight, and handed it to her. At the click of the hand held light, the two gasped simultaneously as the light revealed an ornately detailed and very tarnished brass floor vent. In the center of the vent was a sailboat with a cross adorning its main sail. A circle wrapped neatly around the entire image, including it among the many they had already discovered. "Boone, it's another symbol, isn't it?"

Boone tried to lift the vent from its hole. "Noel, help me!" he struggled. Together, they worked to lift the heavy grate. With his body pressed closely to the covering, the sound of the water was clearer than before. "On three," Boone instructed. "One...two...three." The two pulled at the large square, opening the floor to obscurity below.

Boone shined his light down into the gap, and then pulled himself to where he could see into the opening. Blood rushed to his head making him dizzy and disoriented. Feeling faint, he closed his eyes. The sound of franticly buzzing bees pushed out every other sound around him. The beehive, the Bible, a hand pointing down from heaven, and the voices - they all jammed together and overcrowded his head. His mind floundered as he tried to piece each individual detail together like a giant puzzle. "This can't be real," he tried to assure himself. "What's happening?"

"Are you okay? Boone? Are you all right?" Noel pleaded as she pulled his body away from the vent. "Boone?"

"Huh?" He grinned.

"Are you okay? You blacked out on me and almost fell in head first! What did you see down there? Water?" Noel eagerly begged.

"Books, Noel. I saw lots of books," he stammered.

"Books?"

He turned to his back so she could see that he was sane. "Noel! We found the library!"

She grabbed the flashlight from his hand and sat down on the edge of the opening allowing her legs to dangle down into the unknown. "Lower me in."

"Are you sure? We don't even know what all could be down there! There could be one hundred year old spiders or something." He was thinking that there actually might be one hundred year old people down there who found it fun to mess with his head. Boone decided to keep those thoughts to himself.

"Listen, I have been sleepwalking to my attic for a week now! If I wake up in that dust covered place one more time, I think I'm going to scream. We are going to find the Mishpachah even if it kills me."

Boone was stunned that she hadn't told him about the sleepwalking. "Why didn't you tell me?"

She shrugged. "I don't know. I was restless, maybe upset. I figured I just had too many things to think about, until you told me about your nightmares. Jeff suggested that I ought to work things out with you and maybe that would help me sleep."

"Wait! He knew you were sleepwalking and I didn't?" Boone felt like jealousy had stabbed him again with the idea that Jeff would actually know something about her that he didn't.

"It's not important, lower me down," she said flashing the light on Boone before dropping the flashlight down into the opening. "We're wasting time! Here, take my hands." Boone clutched her wrists and lowered her petite frame into the hole of the store closet floor. He held his breath as she disappeared into the darkness of the room below.

The *pound pound* of a fist broke his concentration. Her hands slipped out of his. "Boone? Noel?" Jeff's voice called out coolly.

"I will come for you. I promise," Boone called down to her. "Turn off your flashlight for a few seconds."

"Boone!" Noel squealed with delight, "I'm standing on something...I think it's a desk. Ouch!"

"Noel? Are you hurt?" he called down frantically, but she didn't answer back.

"I can hear you in there Boone. Is Noel alright?" Jeff asked troubled.

"Sounds like he's really worried about her," Boone thought as he pushed the cardboard box back in front of the floor opening. "I'll be right there."

"Come on, Boone," Jeff demanded.

. Boone leapt to the door and turned the knob, but it was stuck. "I can't. It's locked."

He heard the faint jingle of keys on the other side and then the door swung wide open. "Where's Noel?"

"Last time I saw her she was looking for you," he said truthfully. "Where'd you get the keys?"

Jeff obviously ignored Boone's question and stepped into the room to look around. His eyes moved to the disturbed box and then to Boone. "She's not here."

"Really?" Boone snapped. He needed Jeff to leave so he could get back to Noel. He was nervous about her being down there alone in the dark.

Jeff walked out the door, bumping Boone on the shoulder as he passed. He turned back to face Boone. "What are you doing in here, Boone? Seems like I keep running into you in the strangest places. Anything I should know about?"

"Just need some time to myself, Jeff. Soul searching. Yep, I've been soul searching."

"Be careful where you search, Boone. You might not like what you find."

Boone's bitterness swelled as Jeff shut the door behind him. "I've already found something I don't like."

Chapter 7

Boone's cheeks flushed with anger towards Jeff. Never in his life had he disliked someone so much. In the past week, Jeff's mystery, his charm with Noel, and now his arrogance had become more noticeable to him. Jeff was able to keep calm, even when Boone wanted to knock him down. There was something about Jeff that he disliked so much, but yet there was part of him that Boone wished he could be.

Boone turned back into the tiny storage closet, shut the door behind him, and shoved the cardboard box away from the open vent. "Noel... Noel? Can you hear me?" He waited a few seconds anticipating her response. He called again, "Noel? Are you okay?"

The sound of rushing water seeped through the opening as he awaited her voice. "Get down here Boone! This is amazing!" Her voice was a welcomed relief. Boone scooted his body closer to the vent allowing his feet to hang into the hidden library below. With his hands pressed firmly on the edges, he descended his body until he was standing steadily on a flat surface. A red glow illuminated his contently seated friend. Noel sat crossed leg among stacks of the red leather books, her flashlight rested beside her, and her face was beaming. "We did it! We found it Boone! Look around. It's wonderful."

Noel took her flashlight and shined it slowly around the room. Boone followed the light as it highlighted walls of limestone rock. Resting securely against the walls were towers of heavy wood shelving. Each shelf was neatly organized with red books - exactly like the one he and Noel had found in her attic a week ago. The light shined at his feet. "Watch your step," she warned. Under his feet, a large wooden desk filled the space at the middle of the room. Behind the desk, a leather-backed armchair provided an easy way for him to step down. Each step left his footprint in the carpet of dust that covered the antique piece of furniture. As he balanced with his hand on the back of the chair, Boone smiled cleverly at a wax candle and an open tin box of matches. He sat down comfortably in the old armchair and gave a fleeting look to his surroundings. He breathed in the musty, stale air and pulled a match from its box and attempted to strike it on the side of its tin casing. A hint of sulfur escaped the stick, but as hard as he tried it wouldn't light. He reached for another, this time sifting through the narrow pieces of wood to the bottom of the bunch. Boone struck the box again expecting the same result. To his surprise, he now held a warm glow in his hands that he quickly transferred to the wick of the yellowish candle. The room came to life as the speck of fire flickered and illuminated the four walls.

Boone shivered from the chill of the room on his short-sleeved arms. Blowing hot air into his cupped hands, he warmed them for a second. Then he leaned back in the chair and rested his head against the back. "This has to be part of the original building," Boone gathered, speaking for the first time since his descent.

"Boone, this isn't just a part of the old building. It's *the* library! We're here Boone! Look, it's printed into every one of these books - at least the dozen or so that I have checked," she stammered excitedly. She eagerly flipped through book after book, examining their spines, their covers, and the golden symbols that embellished each one.

He stood to his feet and began to walk the perimeter of the room, stopping in front of her confused. "Why did they hide it? I mean, who would build right over this? Why not add to it? Or…I don't know, how about build a new library and move all of this stuff? Oh, here's an idea, if you don't want anyone to find it, get rid of it." Boone continued to walk and look curiously at each piece of limestone rock, at each intentionally organized book, and every detail that made up this room.

Across from the desk, Boone stopped in front of a framed portrait nestled on a shelf. He looked at the desk behind him and then at the picture in front of him. "Someone once sat here, Noel. Someone sat at that desk and looked at this picture. It must have been important to them if they wanted to look at it everyday." Boone lifted the black and white photograph from its perch and blew many years worth of dust from the glass. A much simpler version of the church loomed at the heart of the picture. There was no steeple, or columns. There was no landscaping or stained glass on the large brick building, but it made sense that this could have been the original meetinghouse of the church.

Boone studied the large number of adults standing proudly in front of the church building. The women were all dressed in long skirts and pristinely pressed blouses. The men were as neatly put together in suit coats and slacks. Each man in the picture wore a jacket and some sported hats. A few children were dotted throughout the congregation. In the middle of the group was a man dressed much like the others, with the exception of a straw wide brimmed hat upon his head and his arm lovingly resting around a woman holding a baby. Instantly, Boone recognized the man in the hat, his eyes, his earthen smell, and most of all his words, "You are him."

He tried to remember each detail of their encounter in the school gymnasium as he studied the portrait. Boone focused on the man first, and then he moved his attention to the lady by his side. She looked familiar, but he was sure that he had never had an encounter with her. He turned the frame over and read aloud the names that had been written on the back, "James Johnson, Nancy Johnson…"

"Nancy Johnson! Her grave is behind the church. When was the picture taken?" Noel asked surprised.

"I don't know, a long time ago?" Boone continued to read, "John Taylor Jr., Violet Covington, Reverend Craig Covington, Ginnifer Covington…"

"Boone stop!" Noel was promptly on her feet and by his side. "Let me see that! That baby is Ginny Covington! That's Jeff's grandmother!" It was clear why the reverend and the lady beside him looked so familiar. The younger version of his assembly visitor looked exactly like Jeff and the lady resembled the church organist, Jeff's grandmother. Noel took the picture to where it could be better seen by candlelight. "I thought so," she uttered seriously returning to the corner where Boone had first seen her. She picked up one of the books she had left open, closed the cover, and presented it to Boone. "They match!"

Boone looked closer at the church photo and then over at the book. Hanging neatly around the neck of Ginnifer Covington's mother was a tiny necklace. From that necklace, there hung a metal circle. Imprinted in that circle was a tree. Its branches were full and round, extending out in every direction, and its roots almost as full pushing downward. Boone ran his fingers over the inscription on the book cover, and read "The Privileges Entrusted to the Leader of the Called Out Ones. Noel, this is the symbol that will lead us to the Mishpachah. I know it!"

"It's the tree of life, Boone," Noel said catching Boone's gaze. "A lot of religions use it to represent family." She stopped for a minute, "Boone…Mishpachah is Hebrew for family! The people in this picture weren't just church people, they were family."

"We have to get back to the windows," Boone exclaimed.

"I agree!" Hurriedly, she stacked a few of the books she perceived might be of value later. As she laid one on top the other, she was mesmerized by symbol after symbol. Each one was elegantly inlaid in gold on the cherry red covers. Boone slid over to extinguish the candle flame, but was distracted by the sound that had drawn them to the vent initially. Noel climbed on the desk, gently pushing the books ahead of her. "Come on, Boone. We have to go."

"Wait a minute. Where's the water coming from?" Listening closely, Boone heard the sound of moving water all around him. With the candle in hand, he pressed his ear against the stony wall. "It's coming from behind the wall. What do you think it is?"

"It could be a stream or something. All of the town's water comes from an underground spring system."

Boone's brain was still processing. "That is the only part of this that makes sense. I've been here my entire life. I have attended church every Sunday and Wednesday since I was born; I even live across the street. Why am I now discovering this? Do you think my parents know? How could nobody have even talked about this?"

"We can worry about that later," she said anxiously. "Help me out!"

Boone blew out the flame and cupped his hands for Noel's foot. With a nudge, he easily hoisted her up into the storage room opening. He waited behind to look around at the hidden library feeling an unusual longing to stay. Something about the elaborate hole made him feel protected.

He followed Noel and lifted his arms to the opening above. Her hands clutched his and pulled him back into the storeroom. The sound of chatter from the fellowship hall carried its way through the door. "Boone, what are we going to do?" Noel asked, dusting the collected dust off her blue jeans. "Did you forget? I'm not supposed to be in here!"

"I have an idea, maybe not a very good one, but it's an idea." Boone knew that he had to get Noel out without being seen. As for himself, he really didn't care as long as he found the window that matched the necklace worn by Ginny Covington. He hoped the blessing on the food had not been given yet. "Wait here," he whispered to her while attempting to squeeze his way out of the closet.

"Hey B!" The overly calm voice of Reed surprised him. "We've been looking for you. Have you seen N? J's been looking all over for her. She totally missed the game." Boone shook his head barely comprehending the concoction of initials Reed had thrown to him. "Well everyone," Reed shouted, "let's eat!"

"Oh wait!" Boone interrupted. "Don't we need to pray first?"

"Guess you weren't paying attention during prayer time now were you mister?" Wayne joked loudly, hoping for a few chuckles from at least a couple youth. Boone's heart sunk. He needed the opportunity of quiet with heads bowed and eyes closed to sneak Noel out of the closet.

"Uh, Reed, I want to pray," Boone choked. He had never once offered to pray in front of anyone.

"Sure, why not!" Reed agreed. It wasn't often he could get any of the teens to pray openly. Boone hoped he wouldn't expect this from him very often.

"Okay, um, let's pray. So, close your eyes, and…um… think about…um…things to be thankful for." Listening for the light scraping of the door opening, he peeked up to see if anyone was looking around. "Oh Lord," he started, "I'm so thankful for the food we are about to eat…" Boone glanced back, but the door remained closed. "And…um…Reed, and the youth group." Hoping to give her time, he continued, "I am also thankful for my mom and dad." This produced a couple chuckles from the hungry group. "And…um…I know that everyone here has things they are thankful for too. So we're gonna tell You." He waited for someone else to speak up, but no one volunteered. Then Boone heard the soft voice of Noel call out the word "friends" confirming her escape to safety.

"Amen!" Boone said loudly. "Let's eat!"

"What was that all about?" Case asked piling his plate with three slices of sausage and bacon pizza.

"I'll tell you later."

"I've known you a long time and never once have you offered to pray, that was weird."

Boone turned around at the voice of Jeff quizzing Noel, "So, where were you?"

"I was looking for you. Where did you go?" she asked strategically holding to the truth.

"I was around, trying to find you and Boone."

"Oh," Noel said at a loss for words and hoping he would change the subject. "I'm sorry I missed the game. I sure hope they have pepperoni and pineapple pizza!" Boone watched them fill their plates and sit at a long folding table with a few of the other youth, three tables away from where they always sat together. An hour ago it would have bothered Boone that Noel wasn't sitting with him, but now, he was glad to have Jeff distracted.

Boone ducked back into the closet, stuffed the books in his pack, and stepped back into the large room. Unexpectedly, he came face-to-face with his two friends. Their arms were crossed ready for answers. "So, what's up?" Wayne questioned, still chewing on a bite of his dinner.

"I'll explain in a minute," Boone said restlessly looking around. The three boys sat down by themselves at a table in the back corner of the fellowship hall. This was their custom at nearly every youth event, but this time, Boone had a specific motive behind his evasiveness.

Boone tried the best he could to explain everything: the symbols, the voices in his head, the dreams, the books, and now the library. In his mind, they should have understood what he was telling them. However, he could tell by the clueless looks on the faces of his friends that his idea of "perfect sense" was not theirs.

Case reached over and placed his freckled hand on Boone's forehead. "No fever. Seriously, this Mishpachah stuff is messin' with your head. It's a fairy tale, Boone."

"Guys, we've been friends a long time. I wouldn't make this up…" Boone stopped talking, giving up on explaining himself. It was time to show hard evidence. He secretively pulled out the book Noel had found in the library.

"Seen it already," Wayne said, starting to get up for more food.

"Wait! Give me another minute. This is a different book. It looks the same, but it's different," he updated them pointing to the tree like symbol on the front cover.

"So what?" Wayne said leaning back in his chair. "It's that old tree by the grave yard."

"What did you say?" Boone asked, looking at the symbol again.

"Oh yeah, I see it," Case exclaimed. "Remember that time we climbed up there to skip church, but your mom caught us. So, you made up that story about being able to hear the sermon better up there. Thanks to you, we've had to sit in front ever since, so *you* could really hear the sermon better."

Boone hadn't recognized the striking resemblance in the tree. How could he have not made the connection? At first it had been another symbol, but now it was real. "Alright then, why did Noel and I find this book in the church library with the shape of that tree on it?"

"Beats me. Didn't even know we had a library," Wayne replied unimpressed.

"There's an opening in the floor of the storage closet! There is a whole library of books under this room!"

"Let's go!" Case encouraged enthusiastically eager to explore.

"Wait! We can't."

"Why not?"

"Because we can't tell anyone about it, not until we find the Mishpachah," Boone said, his voice returning to a whisper. He opened the book, flipped through a couple of pages, and started reading. "The privileges entrusted within are to uphold and protect the body of the Mishpachah. Foremost, to see that the duties of those blessed with the gifts therein are fulfilled. The leadership must hold true to the God designed organization of the body and shroud that which is harmful and unnecessary for the believers."

He stopped there, closed the book, and waited on a response from his childhood friends. Wayne stopped mid-chew. "That book you found really talks about the Mishpachah? It sounds so serious."

Boone knew that he finally had their attention. "These people, whoever wrote all of these red books, knew about the Mishpachah. They have probably even been there…and I think that they may have left behind clues to find it."

Case squinted oddly at Boone. "So what you're saying is that you're going to find the Mishpachah. I thought Noel was nuts!"

"*I'm* not going to find it. We are! Noel and I have already found enough clues to get started. I couldn't let you guys miss out on this one. What do you say?"

Simultaneously, Case and Wayne smiled at each other and said, "We're in!"

Boone felt a boost of confidence and he liked it. "First we find this," he said pointing to the ornate design of their childhood hiding place.

"It's outside," Wayne said smartly.

He was beginning to lose that self-assurance he had gained seconds before. "I think we are looking for something that looks *exactly* like this, roots and all, and I know where we should start."

Chapter 8

Boone, Case, and Wayne finished what was left of their pizza and immediately ran up the stairs to the sanctuary. "Case, you look in the downstairs classrooms. Wayne, you go up and I will look down here," Boone instructed quietly. The boys turned on their flashlights and separated in search of the tree of life. The sounds of teen conversation lingered as they entered the place of worship. He knew this meant they had some time to find what they were looking for before they encountered the others.

Boone traveled the exterior aisles of the church looking at each of the windows. "Nothing in here," Case called from a back classroom.

"Negative," Wayne hollered over the balcony railing.

"Keep looking. I know I've seen it before." Boone was sure of it. He had checked every window in the lower portion of the sanctuary with no success. So he decided to go up to the balcony where Wayne was standing.

"Are you sure it's up here?" Wayne asked still looking around.

"It has to be," Boone answered reaching for the journal in his backpack. The sound of raindrops echoed above him on the roof of the church. A sudden blast of thunder caused Boone to drop the notebook. The pelting rain outside picked up velocity and then another boom of thunder shook the church. Lightning flashed and then another clap of thunder echoed outside. The rain was deafening and the clanging of thunder resonated within the walls. Boone bent down to collect the journal when suddenly, the lightning flashed through the windows. There it was - the tree of life, illuminated by the storm's light. "Over here!" he yelled.

Boone studied the drawings he had made of the windows. "Look," Boone said pointing to the journal, "I knew I had seen it before."

"I know my redeemer liveth," Case, who had joined them, read aloud from the nameplate at the bottom of the window. "Isn't that a song?"

"I think it's in the Bible," Wayne suggested. Both Case and Boone eyed him with surprise. "What? I pay attention, sometimes."

"Now what?" Case asked.

"I don't know," Boone answered. "This is where Noel is usually helpful."

"You want me to go down and get her?"

"No! If we go down there," the crash of thunder interrupted him, "if we go down there, we may draw attention. We need to figure this out ourselves. Okay . . . 'I know my redeemer liveth'. Look around. Do you see anything that kind of goes with that? Noel and I had thought about the beehive, but..."

"You guys ever wondered if you could jump from the balcony and swing on that big light fixture?" Case asked not paying attention.

"Case! Focus!"

"Okay, okay . . . I'll go look!" Case was halfway down the stairs when he called back, "Why aren't we looking for the obvious?"

"He's right, you know," Wayne chimed in. "What's the obvious?"

"Obvious," Boone thought aloud. "Obvious redeemer . . . Christ! That's it! Look for a window with a picture of Christ or his name, anything." The boys separated again to search the sanctuary. The windows had been a new element in Boone's life lately, but he couldn't remember seeing a picture of Christ in any of them. He skimmed through his journal just in case.

The sounds of the youth downstairs waned as the storm outside grew louder. Boone hoped that Reed would assume he and the guys had headed home. It wouldn't have been the first time they had left without checking out.

"Hey!" Noel's presence at the top of the stairs startled Boone. "Did I scare you?"

"No . . . of course not," Boone replied catching his breath and pretending that she hadn't frightened him. "So, where's Jeff? He's not with you, is he?"

"Nope. Reed is having all of us call our parents. A flash flood warning is in effect for the area. I guess the creek is rising. Mrs. Morgan picked him up a few seconds ago. We need to go Boone."

"I can't. It's the tree of life, like the book," he said pointing back to the stained glass image. "Look what it says, 'I know my redeemer liveth'. We're looking for something about our redeemer, anything about Christ."

"Nice work Boone! I'm impressed. I'll help. Have you checked the classrooms up here?"

"Not all of them."

Noel pointed to a closed door directly behind Boone. "That one is Mrs. Covington's classroom. I was thinking . . . " A ripple of thunder cut her off as Boone led the way back to the closed classroom. He slowly opened the door to the senior ladies Sunday school room. Wayne and Case had caught sight of them and followed them into the room. "I knew it was here!"

"What's she talking about, Boone? There's nothing on these windows but a star, a pyramid, and some messed up letters."

"They're not messed up, Wayne! They're Greek. I've seen them as part of the Chi Rho before, but never like this."

"The Chi what?" Boone asked.

"The Chi Rho. I took Greek at my old school."

"Of course she did," Case poked at Boone.

"Let her finish," Boone pleaded, not wanting to make the same mistake twice.

"It's seen in the Chi Rho," Noel explained, now shining her flashlight on the symbol of a banner. On the banner were three letters. The first was the capital letter A, the second like a large lower case m, and the third an upside down U. "Some people called it the monogram of Christ or Chrismon. It looks more like an X, which is Greek for Chi, with a P going through the middle. The P is Greek for Rho. Chi and Rho are the first two letters of "Christ" in Greek. The A and the U are the Alpha and the Omega, sometimes used with the symbol. Christ refers to himself in Revelations this way, 'I am the Alpha and the Omega, the First and the Last, the Beginning and the End.' The symbols have been discovered all over the place; Celtic manuscripts, ancient tombs . . . very early persecuted Christians used it in the catacombs. Supposedly legend has it that Constantine the First was struggling to become the emperor and used the symbol at the front of his military guard. After seeing it magically appear to him, he won and became the first Christian emperor of Rome."

"She's so smart," Case teased. "I kind of like that in a girl."

"Knock it off," Boone said pushing him jokingly. "N, what's next?"

"I don't know. The M doesn't make sense. It is the Mu in Greek, and I am pretty sure it actually means the word 'nothing'. I can't see the rest of it. This pew is in the way." An old pew had been painted, padded, and placed in front of the window for comfortable seating. Without being asked, Boone, Case and

Wayne lifted the far end of the long seat out of the way to reveal another blank window.

"I don't understand. Sorry guys. I want this as bad as you but . . . " again her words were cut off as lightning flared and thunder drummed down on them.

"Wait! Did you see that?" Boone was now on his knees in front of the window. "Someone hand me a flashlight!" He took his flashlight and shined it through the window adjacent to the window stained with the Chi Rho. "The light shines through." He then moved the light over to the nameplate under the monogram of Christ. "Like you said Noel, nothing! Something is keeping the light from shining through the glass here. Something is behind the nameplate. This is the one!"

"What are you suggesting? We vandalize the place?" Case asked looking down at Boone.

"Watch out," Wayne said moving swiftly to the window and flipping open his pocketknife. Because he had carried a knife with him everywhere he went since he was five, the appearance of a miniature weapon was not a shock to anyone present.

"Oh no you don't," Noel said halting the process and removing the knife from Wayne's grip. "If anyone is doing this, it's me." She set to work whittling out the glue that held the plate by its edges. "I've almost got it!" The edges of the plate loosened. Noel worked cautiously on the glass plate trying hard not to do any permanent damage. The wind changed directions and the rain began to beat against the windows. Steadily, the rain poured against the pane as she worked. She stopped, sat back on the floor, and gently lifted the plate from its home. A yellowed piece of folded paper drifted slowly down into her lap. She breathed in heavily.

Boone reached down, lifted it up, and peered intently at the crumbling paper. "Noel, get the first book." She shook her arms out of her backpack straps and grabbed the book containing the image of a beehive. She turned the pages until she reached the spot where a page should have been but was curiously missing. Then she softly read the words that she had read to the boys a few days before, "The Reverend Elijah Craig became the pastor of The Great Crossings Baptist church and . . . "

The boys held their breath as Boone gently opened the parchment. He looked at it and then up at the boys. Then he read, ". . . the believers. His legacy lies with His bride, whom he loved and served faithfully. In death, he will be remembered for his accomplishments and his dedication . . . "

"That's enough Boone," Noel said looking up at him with energy in her eyes. "That's it! His legacy is what he was most remembered for, what he left behind - the knowledge of the Mishpachah! Don't you see? He buried the entrance with his wife . . . his bride! I was looking for the wrong grave all along!" Brimming with excitement, she leapt to her feet, grabbed each one, and hugged them.

"Whoa, whoa, whoa! I'm not digging up any dead woman!" Case worriedly remarked.

"He's right. What do we do, Noel?" Boone asked.

"I say that we at least check out the church cemetery again. It would make sense that his wife would be buried beside him, right? And we kind of think he might be in the church cemetery or close by. So, let's see if we can find her headstone. A lot of the tombstones were broken and hard to read. I need a better look."

"You guys up there?" Reed's voice called from the sanctuary below.

Ignoring Reed's call, Wayne asked, "So what happens if we do find this lady's grave? Will some magic door pop up out of the ground?" The teens could now hear Reed's footsteps coming up the stairs.

"I doubt it, but if we can prove that Mrs. Craig is down there, then maybe that will be enough evidence to suggest that Elijah Craig is beside her! That alone should get some of the historians in town to get a team in here to exhume the bodies, and then maybe the entrance will be found. We will be heroes or something," she rambled talking faster and faster.

"What about us? We did all the work? If it's down there, I want to see it!" Case declared.

"He's right, Noel. We have to find it before anyone else. We can't miss this chance," Boone whispered looking at her pleadingly. Boone knew with everything in him that he had to go. No one else could find it before them.

"Are you serious? What if you get hurt, or…worse?" Noel interrogated.

"This was your idea!" Boone jokingly responded.

"Sure, but…" She thrust the dedication plate behind her back and stepped in front of the window as Reed entered the room.

"What are you all up to? Everyone's gone and the storm's getting worse," Reed said suspiciously looking at the four youth.

"We're playing?" Boone answered, shining his flashlight into his own face.

"All right, everyone out," Reed motioned.

Wayne and Case followed Reed out the door. Noel stayed inside to push the bench back against the stained glass window. Boone waited for her by the doorway, but she brushed coldly by him on her way out. "Hey Noel, wait a minute. What was that all about?"

"I don't understand you lately. I know you think you are somehow disconnected from me, and I get it now, but this isn't like you! We have always been a team. People argue, it's normal. I'm over it, so we're good now," Noel stated obviously irked.

"What are you talking about?" Boone asked not understanding his friend's annoyance.

"I know when you said 'we' should be the first to go in, that you really meant you!" Noel bit back.

"Where is this coming from?" Boone begged for an explanation.

"Things are changing. You are changing. The Boone I knew would think this through. The Boone that I knew would stand up for me. Please listen to what I'm saying! I'm your friend! I'm not sure we should even be doing this anymore. Something feels really wrong about it. I mean you're having all these nightmares, or visions, or whatever you call them. Now we are going to be grave robbers? Come on Boone! This was supposed to be fun. Like the time we were archeologists and dug up the back yard. Now it's going too far. Say you do find her grave…what then? Are you really going to start digging? We should get someone that knows what they are doing."

Boone shook his head and replied, "You saw the library. You have read the books, and now stuffed behind a window we find a one-hundred-year-old page from a library book that isn't supposed to exist. We have discovered so much! We can't stop now! I can't do this without your help. You've already had your chance at hanging out in the graveyard, now it's my turn." Noel rolled her eyes.

"Alright," she said smiling at Boone before walking out the door. "Promise me that there will be no digging until we talk about it, okay?"

"Okay," he assured.

Noel looked back at him, "You are him, Boone Tackett. You really are."

He stared at her stunned and now even more confused by her. He was faced with a task he really didn't want to do, but knew that if he didn't he might go mad.

Chapter 9

A soft drizzle of rain remained from last night's storm. The drowsy students sat in the same seats they had chosen on the day they officially were classified as "youth". Boone stared down at his uneaten doughnut. His hunger told him to take a bite, but his exhausted body couldn't quite convince his hands to pick it up. His eyes were heavy from a night of unrest. The sweet smell of icing continued to tempt him until he lifted the chocolate glazed doughnut to his mouth and with his eyes half shut ate the whole thing.

Their recent discoveries scurried around his brain like mice in a maze. Had he and Noel really been in a hidden library the night before? Was that really Jeff's grandmother in the picture? Stranger still, was it her mother's necklace that led them to find the lost page that revealed the location of the Mishpachah? He was having trouble believing that any of it really happened, but he knew what he had to do.

Glancing around, Boone could tell that Case and Wayne were tired. Dark circles had formed under their reddened eyes and their mouths widened in frequent yawns. Noel appeared to be paying attention to Reed's lesson, but occasionally, Boone watched her eyelids falling and then popping open again. They had spent most of the night on the phone planning their mission. No one had wanted to wait another day. Boone would go first.

"So . . . great game of flashlight tag last night gang. Lots of fun! Do we have any prayer requests this morning?" Reed's spunkiness was too much for Boone this early in the morning. Jeff's hand shot up. Boone watched to see if Noel would turn to look at him. "What's up J?"

"My grandmother..." The word grandmother grabbed their attention. Noel, Boone, Case, and Wayne all turned to look at Jeff. "She isn't feeling well; keep her in your prayers."

"Will do. Anyone else? All right, let's open in prayer. Let's see, any volunteers? How about you B?" Reed pointed straight at Boone. He answered by pointing to his mouth full of chocolate goo. "Let's bow our heads," Reed continued agitated.

"Wait, Reed," Noel spoke up, "I do have one. I know it's been a few years since I moved here, but it's still not easy being so far away from everything that I knew. So if you could kind of pray for that, it would be great."

"Really Noel!" Boone nearly shouted. "You call me selfish? Everyday, it's about you! It's always about poor homesick Noel. Shouldn't you be over it by now? People move all the time!" All eyes were on him.

Jeff was on his feet, "Boone, calm down."

"I'm not talking to you, Jeff. This is between us. Go ahead and move back if you hate it here so much Noel!" He slammed his hands down convincingly on the table, stood to his feet, and started to stomp out the door into the misty Sunday morning.

"B, wait!" Reed called after him. "What's going on? You're not yourself lately."

"Everybody keeps saying that," Boone mumbled.

"First the fight with Jeff, and now this. Is there something we need to talk about? You know I'm here for you?"

Boone felt bad that Reed had been dragged into this. He really did know that the college kid before him had the best motives, but the last thing Boone cared to do was share his feelings. "I need to be alone, if that's okay?" Reed patted him on the shoulder and returned to the youth room. Boone had the sneaking suspicion that his mom would be receiving another call from Reed.

Eagerly, Boone ran his hands through his gel encrusted hair and took off towards the church cemetery that was directly ahead of him. Adrenaline from his outburst had given him a sudden energy boost. He hoped everyone had believed the staged fit that allowed him to leave class with no suspicion.

The limestone walls that surrounded the graveyard came up to Boone's chest. There was a time when he couldn't even see over them. For years the walls existed in disorder. In places, it had been completely torn down. Then about four years ago, a team from the Dry Stone Conservancy got together to make the needed repairs. Boone had volunteered to help alongside his dad.

The mist returned to a drizzle. "Terrific," he grumbled. Hesitant to go inside, he continued walking around the walls. He came to a spot where stones had been intentionally placed inside the wall to form a staircase. "That's weird," he thought. He lifted himself onto the wall and stepped down the stairs. "Who puts stairs in a graveyard? Oh yah, probably the same people that bury a library." The ground below his feet was saturated. He could feel the mud beginning to seep in between his toes as he regretted his decision to wear flip-flops to church this morning. The frayed hem of his blue jeans was splattered with specks of mud. "Mom is going to flip out," he groaned. Boone tried to roll his pants up to prevent any further damage. But having no luck, he gave in to the mud and began his search around the graveyard. He was looking for anything with the name Craig, or maybe one of the symbols. The rain was coming down harder now. Nevertheless, he was here and he wasn't going to give up. First, he checked the two obelisk shaped headstones. The taller of the two was fully intact and engraved with the name "Nancy", just as Noel had seen the Wednesday evening before. "Wife of James Johnson . . . died 1850," Boone read to himself. He trudged over to the next one. It would have been the tallest had the top not broken off into pieces. Intently, he studied the mostly worn away writing. It was clear the deceased had been a Johnson. If Noel's husband and wife theory was correct, this could have been James.

Boone continued walking around lifting broken pieces of granite and tombstones along the way. He was fervently looking, hoping, and praying for a clue. There had to be one that would clear everything up. Boone trekked over to where flat slabs of stone lay on the far end of the cemetery. He squatted down, and wiped decade's worth of debris from the surface, but nothing. The church steeple clanged loudly over the screeching of the first bell dismissing Sunday school. The youth would be leaving their class and walking into worship any minute.

To conceal himself from any church arrivals, he sat on a large rock at the back corner of the cemetery and leaned his head against the wall. *There's nothing here! What am I doing?* he questioned himself. Smelling the clean scent of rain, he breathed it in. His ears tuned in to the *drip drip* of water hitting the leaves in the tree above him. Boone wondered if this was where Elijah Craig had sat so many years before. He opened his mouth to taste the fresh rain. He knew that he couldn't go back into the church like this. He was soaking wet and mud splattered. *"I'll wait until church starts. Then, I will run home and change,* he planned.

As the drops sprayed down on his face, he stared up into the branches above him and waited. The cadence of the rain on the stone walls relaxed him until the steeple bells chimed again announcing that service was about to begin. Boone remained patiently silent and motionless. Then, he stood; slowly peeking over the wall to make sure no one would see him as he was walking home. Glancing around one last time, he started his trek toward the staircase that had led him in. Boone stopped moving as a shiver emerged from his toes, ran up his back, and through his heart. The ground below him slightly quivered.

Boone stayed completely still. He knew what that stir was about and the heavy rains the night before were making it even more dangerous. There was more than one reason why children were warned not to play in the graveyard. The entire state of Kentucky was practically resting on the longest series of caves in the world. His parents had warned him not to play in the cemetery where the ground had been loosened and could potentially be unstable. Even when he and his dad had worked on the wall, they were told to be very careful. At one point in the church's history the parking lot had fallen victim to the cave system phenomenon. As a result, a giant crater like sink hole emerged directly on the outside of the front cemetery wall. Holding his breath, he gingerly took a step. The ground moved again. This time he could feel it giving way beneath him. He tried to jump, but the sole of his flip-flop became stuck in the soft mud. He pulled at his leg. It was no use. His foot lodged deeper into the muck. Panic began to take its hold on him. There was not a soul in sight. The wall was close. If he could reach it, maybe he could pull himself free. Boone lunged for the stones ready to leave his shoe behind. The earth shifted again and the ground loosened giving way to the caves below. With arms thrashing in the air, he tried to grab at anything within reach. "Help!" he yelled. Flailing, his body plunged into the darkness below.

Boone gradually opened his eyes. His back ached from its sudden contact with the hard limestone floor beneath him. He warily tried to sit up, but his lower leg was twisted into a position beneath him that he discerned was not normal. As he moved, a sharp stabbing pain in his ankle told him that he was badly injured. He tried to adjust his eyes to the darkness surrounding him so he could assess the area. He had heard stories of kids at school finding entrances to caves in the middle of fields. Once they hiked deeper into it, the cave floor eventually dropped off hundreds of feet. With his arms outstretched, he explored the floor around him to determine the amount of solid space with which he could move. His ankle was now throbbing and something warm was streaming down his cheek. From the opening several feet above a thin beam of light found him and revealed the oozing liquid. "Blood," he exhaled, wiping his wound with the back of his hand. "I must have cut myself when I fell." Relief flooded through him as he appreciated that at least he was still alive. Tiny drops of rain fell through the open earth. Cupping his hand, Boone tried to catch them to clean the wound on his face. It stung to touch. He extended his hands up again, but the rainwater stopped and his bit of light disappeared.

"Is he down there?" inquired the voice of a young girl. Boone's heart jumped.

"Help!" he called.

"I can't see him. Do you hear anything?"

"I'm down here!" he yelled with what breath had been left to him.

"Bubby? Is that you?"

Boone would never have imagined that he would appreciate the squeaky voice of his sister, but here, it was the most pleasant sound he had ever heard. "Yes! Get help Kaylee!"

"You all right?" Wayne's face was vaguely apparent in the opening above. "I'm coming down."

"No, wait. I don't know what's down here." Boone's words were silent to Wayne. Wayne tossed a flashlight, left behind from the prior night's youth event, down into the dark pit. Boone turned on the light and shined it on the silhouette of the descending Wayne.

"Easy Case! If you drop me, you're a dead man. Well, Boone might be if I land on him." Wayne's feet were the first thing Boone could see. Once Wayne made it safely on the ground, Boone shined the light around to see that their surface space was truly big enough for the both of them. "Are you hurt?"

"Huh? Oh yah. My ankle is busted and I think the cut on my face is bad." Wayne took the flashlight from Boone and shined it on his left cheek.

"That looks kind of nasty. Let's get you out of here."

"Wait Wayne, look!" The light from the flashlight revealed that what he had assumed was a cave was actually a room similar in size and shape to the library he and Noel had found the day before. Instead of shelves filled with books, the shelves were larger and filled with intricately carved wooden caskets stacked five high.

"Get me out! I am not into dead people! Hey Case . . . "

"Hush Wayne…even if it means finding the Mishpachah?"

Before Wayne had a chance to answer, Noel's voice became clear as she was the next to be lowered in. "Catch me guys." Noel descended next, followed by Kaylee. Then, making an educated jump was Case.

"Kaylee! What are you doing here? You shouldn't be here! You could've been hurt or killed! Guys, how could you let her come?"

Noel stepped between the feuding siblings. "That's enough you two. Boone, she's the one that saw you falling. She came to get us . . . and she said she would tell if we didn't."

"But how did you know Kaylee?"

"You weren't with the guys after Sunday school and you're always with the guys. I checked downstairs and then I came out here. I heard you scream, but I couldn't see you. So I got the boys and Noel," she said smiling.

"Seriously, someone should have stayed topside to get us out," Boone suggested.

"I wrote a note Boone," Kaylee chimed in.

"A note?"

"Yep! I left a note in our seats to tell mom where we were going. That's what I'm supposed to do when I go out to play Boone!"

Boone reached out for her and embraced her in his arms, "Thank you, Kaylee!"

"Boone Tackett, we are going to settle this once and for all," Noel demanded fiercely. Then, she beamed, "That was awesome! I had no idea what you were going to say when I mentioned that whole homesick thing. I wish you hadn't gotten

Jeff involved though. Reed was so shaken all he could say was, 'He needs to cool off a bit'."

"You were good, maybe you should take up acting," Wayne joked. "I think I would have faked sick or something."

"I don't exactly feel great about it," Boone said feeling guilty for deceiving Reed.

"Alright, let's get on with this. Church will be over in about forty-five minutes. They'll be looking for us," Case said surveying the room. "So, which one is the bride?"

"Everyone, start looking," Boone instructed. "We need more light!" Noel reached inside her floral print backpack and pulled out another flashlight. It was the one Jeff had let her borrow. "Thanks," he winked at her.

"No problem," Noel replied sarcastically. The group of five searched the room with what faint light they had. "Martha Tackett, Leader," she read aloud. "Hey guys, look!" The group gathered around the wooden casket. "It's a symbol from the church windows." The image of the Bible that Boone had seen exactly one week ago was perfectly whittled into the coffin under the word "Keeper".

"Noel!" Kaylee shouted. "They all have names and goofy shapes on them." Each wooden casket held the name of the deceased and a word like keeper, musician, leader, or gardener. Inscribed under each word was one of the symbols from the stained glass church windows. The teens were baffled at the existence of an underground tomb, but more so at the awkwardness of the inscriptions.

"None of these have the name Craig on them anywhere!" Boone grumbled disappointedly.

"What do we do now?" Wayne asked.

"I don't know. This doesn't make any sense. He should be here!"

"Wait, what's that?" Case investigated, knocking clumps of fallen mud from his already dirty hair. The earth above them started to crumble.

The teens quickly huddled together in the corner of the room. The roar of stone and dirt falling from above grew louder as more and more came down upon them. "I'm scared!" Kaylee cried.

"These walls have been here a long time. They're not going to hold!" Wayne informed. As the earthen ceiling gave way, the broken tombstones came crashing down from the cemetery above. A few of the wooden caskets were knocked over and lids popped open.

The dust settled leaving the light from the two flashlights illuminating a new wall of dirt and broken shelving. "I think it stopped," Boone commented as he attempted to maneuver around his friends in what scarce space had been left to them.

"Hey guys, look! The coffins are empty," Case said observing one of the dust filled open caskets. "What is this place anyway?"

"I'm not sure," Boone answered examining his surroundings once again. "But whatever it is, we're here to stay…at least for a while."

Chapter 10

The tomb was dark even with the flashlights that Noel and Wayne held in their hands. Kaylee had taken a seat on a fallen rock; her pink cotton dress stained a blackish brown. Case and Wayne had begun an attempt to dig their way out, making no real progress. Noel inspected the limestone walls and the wooden caskets that had not fallen during the cave in. Boone hobbled to where Kaylee was sitting and put his arm around her.

"It's my fault," she whined. "If I had told mom and dad, we wouldn't be stuck here."

"Kaylee, this isn't your fault. I was looking around where I wasn't supposed to be, this is my mistake." With his chin resting on her head, he was able to smell her strawberry shampoo scented hair. "Besides, mom and dad will find your note and everything will be okay. We'll be home in no time." The idea of rescue loomed in the air, but was realistically very far away. Occasionally, bits of dirt and rock fell from the ground above them. The more Wayne and Case dug, the more rubble fell.

"I think we should stop," Wayne said worriedly. "The rest of this could come down on us."

"You're right. Let's sit here and wait," Boone agreed, keeping his arm around his frightened sister. The other boys found spots against the wall and sat to rest.

"Boone, could you come here a sec?" Noel called. He kissed Kaylee on the cheek and went over to a piece of wall that had not been used to house the empty caskets.

"What's up?"

"Recognize this symbol?" She pointed to where etched into stone was the beehive. "Boone! This is it. This is the same symbol that was on the front of the first book we found. The one about Elijah Craig! This has to be where he is buried. If not him, his bride will have to be here! You were right about the beehive Boone! This must be the way!"

Boone grinned from ear to ear, his spirit of adventure overriding his aches and pains. "Let's open it!"

"I can't. It's solid."

The wall appeared to be thick with no sign of a doorway or opening. "You don't think his body will be back there do you?" Boone asked uneasily.

"Actually, no. Even if this is his tomb, none of the caskets had a single bone in them. His tomb would probably be empty as well. Besides, we're not looking for dead bodies. We're looking for the Mishpachah!" Noel stated emphatically.

Boone stopped her. "Listen, do you hear it? Put your ear close to the wall."

Noel gave him a skeptical look and then put her ear to the symbol. "It's water! It's louder than what we heard last night in the library, and it's moving faster."

"I know, but there is another sound. I can't make it out."

"Boone," Noel whispered to him without letting the others hear, "this may or may not be the way to the Mishpachah. But if there is an underground stream on the other side of this wall, it may lead us out! We won't make it too long under here. There's not enough oxygen for all five of us. We have to move!"

"What are you suggesting?" Boone said warily. "We bust through the wall and follow the river?"

"The whole town's water supply comes from an underground spring system," Noel reminded him. "That has to be the spring! We follow it and it will take us right out into town. We can do this Boone!"

"All right, but you're explaining this one to Wayne and Case."

"They won't listen to me. They'll find some way to make a joke out of it. You do it . . . "

"Do what?" Case interrupted.

"Break through the wall and follow the spring on the other side," Boone answered.

"Break down the wall?" Case asked for clarity.

"I am so in!" Wayne interjected.

Instantly, Kaylee was on her feet. "But Bubby, the whole place will fall in! Please don't let them! Let's wait."

"All right," Noel was standing firm and ready for diplomacy. "All those in favor of going through the wall say 'aye'."

The "ayes" of Case, Wayne, and Noel rang out. Boone didn't want to upset Kaylee even more, so he just nodded his head in agreement.

The four pushed with shoulder and arms pressing against the wall. "It's . . . not . . . moving," Wayne grunted.

"On three, everyone pushes harder," Boone instructed. "One . . . two . . . threeeee!" They pushed with all the strength they could find in them, but the wall stood firm. Wayne wiped the sweat from his forehead with the palm of his hand and then placed it on the wall for balance. "Gross! What is this?"

Noel shined the flashlight on his hand. It was covered in a powdery gray substance and the symbol was now smeared. She scratched a few times at the symbol, and then at the wall. "Wayne, toss me your knife." She carefully scraped away at the symbol until there was a circular opening in the wall.

"What now?" Boone asked.

89

"Stick your hand in it," Case suggested.

"What!"

"I saw it in a movie once. Stick your hand in it!" he said excitedly.

Boone looked over at Noel. "Couldn't hurt," she giggled.

He stalled by pretending to inspect the front of the opening. Then, he gradually slid his hand into the dark hole. "What the…" he shouted jumping back. His hand was dripping with sticky goo.

"Disgusting!" Wayne mumbled.

A sweet smell immediately filled the room. "Bubby, I smell honey!" Kaylee beamed. Boone sniffed the foreign substance. Sure enough, he had stuck his hand in a hole of sweet honey.

"It's honey Noel!" Boone laughed joining in with the others. "It's honey! What do I do with it?"

His question stopped the laughter and brought the group back to the uncertainty of their situation. "It has to be a clue of some sort," Noel assessed. "Honey? Wait a minute! The land flowing with milk and honey! Oh course! God told Moses he would deliver the Israelites from the Egyptians and that he would deliver them to land flowing with milk and honey!"

"So, what did they have to do to get there?" Case asked.

"They wandered in a desert for forty years," Noel suggested.

"I'm not staying down here for forty years. No way! I have a Christmas concert to prepare for!" Case exploded.

"Then, they had to bring down the wall of Jericho," Noel continued.

"Oh, oh, I know this one," Kaylee said jumping up and down. "They had to march around the city for six days and they had to blow their trumpets. Then after that, they marched one more time and had to scream really loud. Then, the wall came down."

Boone, Wayne, Case, and Noel looked at each other. Then at the top of their lungs, they all screamed,

"AAAAHHHHHHH." When nothing happened, they replaced their screams with a disappointed groan.

"Listen," Boone instructed. "That noise, it's growing louder. I can't make it out, but I think it's... BEES!" A swarm of bees gushed forth from the hole and frantically flew around the room. The group swatted at the pests. Terrified, they covered their faces and curled up into balls on the ground. The sound of the swarming bees was resounding. Then the noise ceased and the bees were gone. The group slowly stood to their feet. Boone hobbled to the now empty hole and listened. "They're not in here. Is everyone okay? Did anyone get stung?" Of the entire group, not a person had even a red mark or sting on them. Boone stared deep into the hole. "I think I see something! It's a handle of some sort!"

Noel grinned at him and then reached for the handle. She gripped the sticky metal and turned it to the right. As she turned, the stones began to crack forming a rectangular door. "Guys, help me push!" The boys ran and pushed at the now visible doorway. The ceiling above them started to move. Pebbles were falling. "Push harder!" With their effort, it broke loose and swung open revealing an enormous cavern.

"Kaylee, let's go!" Boone screamed over the falling dirt and rocks.

"I'm afraid Bubby!" She sat frozen. Wayne, Case, and Noel ran through the open entry. Boone ran towards his sister and lifted her in his arms. She buried her tear stained face in his chest as he leaped through the doorway. As they crossed the threshold, the entrance filled with stone, rock, and soil.

It was as if they had literally walked through a wall and into a whole new world. The five were amazed at the massiveness of the cave walls that surrounded them. The undisturbed cavern walls glistened and reflected the light from the teens' hand-held illuminations. Their shadows towered above them in the cold thick air. The only sounds they could hear were the rushing of water - and their own deep breathing. While admiring the grandness of the area, Boone became aware of the swiftness of the two narrow rivers that ran on each side of them.

"We did it! We really did it!" Noel yelled. The teens cheered and hugged one another. Amazed by their discovery, everyone forgot for a moment that they had no idea where they were. Throughout the hall of limestone, their voices carried and bounced off the walls, accompanying the roars of the water. "Our screaming released the bees! The movement of the bees must have exposed the handle! We did it!"

Boone's growling stomach disturbed his excitement. He wished he had eaten more than a doughnut that morning. He limped to the water's edge, crouched down, and scooped up the clear water. The clean liquid tasted refreshing and free of chemicals and water treatments. He drank again and again. By now, the others had anxiously joined him.

"What now?" Wayne asked looking directly at Boone. All eyes were on him as if he were a map to their rescue.

"Why are you all looking at me?" he asked curiously.

"What do we do?" Kaylee asked him.

Boone couldn't figure out why everyone looked to him to make the decision. It wasn't like he was in charge of their expedition. What if he made the wrong decision and they were stuck in the cave? What if he stepped over the edge of an invisible cliff and the whole group followed him right over the edge, but no one else seemed to be making a move. "I, uh, I guess we follow the river," he suggested unsure of himself, but recognizing it was probably the only option they had.

Without hesitation, Noel took the lead and followed the flow of the streams. Boone kept near the back of the group; he didn't want to be in charge. He prayed that he hadn't steered them into danger as he watched her walk away. As much as he loved adventure, he loved his friends more.

As his friends moved on, Boone found that he was left behind in the darkness of the cave. He could see the dimness from their flashlights fading, so he picked up his pace in order to catch up with them. He had experienced what the absence of light would be like, and even if it was a dream, he didn't want to experience it again. A dull throbbing was beginning at the base of his neck and working its way to the top of his head. He couldn't think straight and suddenly couldn't make sense of anything that had happened that day, especially how he was feeling right now. The uneasy sensation in his stomach had morphed into prickles of pain and slowed him down. "*You,*" he heard around him. "*You are him.*" He wasn't in the mood for this now. The voice was growing louder. "*You, you are him.*" The others had unknowingly gone ahead of him. He tried to walk faster, but the voice and its effects were slowing him down.

He stopped to take another sip of water. "Wait!" he yelled to stop the group. Boone knew something was wrong, and he was afraid of being left behind. Kaylee ran back to him with her long tangled curls bouncing behind her.

"Bubby, are you all right?"

"Yah, I'm fine . . . a little hungry, but I'm fine." The feeling was more than hunger; it was an emptiness that ate at him every time it spoke. Kaylee knelt beside him.

"Are you okay, Boone? You don't look so good," Noel asked worried.

"We need to go back," Boone tried to moan. "We have to go back."

"That's ridiculous! There's nothing back there, Boone. They can't find us in a room that's not there anymore. This is our best shot."

"We were supposed to eat the honey. We wasted it. It was our food," he tried to breathe out.

Noel placed her hand on his forehead. "You aren't making sense, and you're burning up Boone! You don't know what you are saying. Guys, we have to rest a minute. He's not well!"

"No!" Boone shouted with sweat pouring down his face. "We are going the wrong way! There's another way! We need food! We have to get to the honey!"

"It's okay Boone. We can't go back, but we can eat." Noel smiled at him sympathetically not knowing what else to do. He watched through blurred vision as she dug through the contents of her backpack. He could see the red leather books and her Bible. Boone remembered how she always carried her Bible and how he admired that. Friends at school often made fun of her. He wished he had defended her more. "Here," she said handing him a few M&M's and some Combos. "I had these in my bag. We can share. It's not much, but it will help. We should be a couple miles outside of town." The bag of candy and cheese-filled pretzel tubes were passed around the group until they were empty.

The few bites of food helped his pounding head, but he knew something wasn't right. He had a peculiar feeling like something really bad was about to happen if they kept going. It was almost as if some kind of internal compass had been implanted inside of him, telling him that there was another way.

"Bubby look!" Kaylee squealed excitedly pointing and jumping up and down. Boone looked in the water to see what it was that had caught her attention. "It was a fish Boone! It was white and it was really big!" The water itself appeared black in the darkness of the cave.

"You're tired Kay. We all are. You're seeing things."

"I saw it Boone. I really did!"

Wayne inched closer to Kaylee. "You know, some people say the fish that live in these caves are blind. It's so dark in here that they don't even need eyes."

"How do you know that?" Kaylee questioned.

"My mom used to tell me stories about these caves. I have caves like this under the farm, not this big, but they're caves all right. So, it's possible that you really did see one. Right, Boone?" Wayne asked, calming Kaylee and bringing Boone back to reality.

"Right," he answered. He really did appreciate Wayne's help.

Kaylee took Wayne's hand hoping he would have more fun stuff to tell her about big fish and hidden caves. Boone didn't feel anywhere close to normal, but he knew he couldn't sit in the dark by himself doing nothing. He followed slowly at the back of the group, noticing how occasionally one of them would glance behind to see if he was still there. He tried hard to not let his mind wonder, but it seemed to ease his pain to think about something else. He wondered when the last time was that someone had traveled between these two waters, or if anyone had ever traveled them at all. He wondered if he stayed down here long enough if he'd no longer need his eyes and go blind like the fish. He wondered if they would ever get back home.

Not knowing where they would end up, Noel, Case, Wayne, Kaylee, and Boone followed the streams. Inside, they each held onto the hope of what they might find. Case and Wayne schemed about what they would do once they became famous for finding the Mishpachah. Noel and Kaylee chatted about Noel's former church. Boone tried to listen to the voices of his friends and not the persistent one echoing inside of him. He was sure that several hours had already passed by, but because no one was wearing a watch or had a phone, there was no way to know what time it was. Every mile of the cave wall was different. Some were glossy and shimmering, others cut deep into the earth producing jagged edges that the travelers avoided. Despite their differences, they all started to look the same to Boone. He felt like they might be walking in one huge circle.

"Let's stop to rest for a few minutes," he spoke up.

"Yah, good idea," Noel commented. No one really needed a rest, but everyone sat for a minute because they knew that Boone did.

Kaylee jumped back to her feet and ran to the water's edge. "Bubby! There it is! I see it! It's the white fish!" Boone watched as his inquisitive sister bent at the waist, and leaned into the larger of the two streams.

"Kaylee! You're too close!" he yelled, but it was too late.

"Boone!" Kaylee cried, her arms splashed wildly in the black cave river. "Help!" The water quickened as if her presence was pushing it deeper into the darkness of the cave. The echoes of her screams were an uncomfortable comfort that she might be okay.

Chapter 11

Boone hesitated, not knowing what to do. "Go in after her!" Noel screamed to him.

"What?" Boone called back.

"Don't just stand there! Go!"

Shock immobilized Boone. It wasn't that he didn't want to go, he was afraid to go. He knew that he had to go in after her. The voices swirled in his head again. He waited to see which of his friends were preparing to dive in, but they were watching frantically anticipating his move. Briefly, he blacked out. Then, he felt his body being pushed into the obscurity of the underground river. The iciness burned at his skin and swiftly brought him back to the severity of his sister's dilemma. It moved him faster than his arms could pull his body. "Kaylee!" he screamed. He wouldn't allow himself to think of anything else but her. She was nowhere in sight. The others ran alongside the water's edge frantically shining their flashlight beams into the pitch of the water. "Kaylee!" Boone screamed again.

His bare toes scraped against the water worn bottom of the river floor. Half swimming and half flailing, he swam with every ounce of courage in him. As he opened his mouth to scream again, he gulped in the cave water. Choking and gasping for air, fear began to creep into him. The 'what ifs' were pouring through him faster than his brain could process as he thought the worst of what might have happened. *She's alive*, he tried to convince himself. *I have to believe she's still alive!*

His sides cramped and his ankle seared in pain with every kick. *Oh Lord*, he begged, *not Kaylee, please not her!* Alone in the cold current of the water, anguish and despair threatened his sanity. *I'll do anything, Lord, anything!* Boone had said this empty prayer to the Lord many times. But this time, he meant it and he was willing to do anything to save his sister.

The flashlights continued to illuminate areas of the widening river. Occasionally, one of the lights would fall back on him and then return ahead of him. The geography of the cave was changing. The walls were becoming rough and darker, marking the way to some scary and unknown place. Boone could hear Noel's voice echoing, "Kaylee! We're coming!"

He closed his eyes and pleaded one more time, *Anything Lord*. Boone had no doubt that God had heard his plea. He wanted – no *needed* - an immediate answer. Patience had never been one of his strong points, especially not now. Kaylee was still not visible and her screams were no longer heard. In spite of his aching arms, pounding chest, and turning stomach, he pushed on, but he was unconfident as to whether or not he had the strength to keep going.

"*You are him, Boone.*" Oddly, the usually unwelcomed voice brought comfort. "*You are him.*"

"Boone!" The more familiar voice brought him slowly out of his stupor and allowed him to focus on the dim light of his friends. "Do you see her, Boone?" Feeling dazed, he couldn't make out the voice. He thought it might be Wayne or Case. "She's right in front of you!" He feverishly groped around in the water until he found the shivering arm of a fearful girl. Relief coursed through him as he clutched it and pulled himself tightly to her.

"Bubby," she whimpered.

"I need light!" he yelled to his friends. His sister held tightly to a stone formation that protruded out of the water a few feet from the water's edge. She was trembling uncontrollably. Her wet hair clung to her face and her body was cold to his touch. Despite his waning strength, he managed to hold her with one arm and the formation with the other.

"Give me your hand!" Wayne yelled to Kaylee. Frightened, she shook her head and clenched her arms more tightly around Boone.

"Don't leave me Bubby," she sobbed.

"It's going to be okay. Wayne's right there. He's the tallest and he can reach you if you let go."

"No Bubby, please. I'm so afraid."

"Trust me on this. It's going to be all right. When we get home . . . "

"We're going home, Boone?"

"Of course! Now reach out your hand." Warily, the shivering body reached out her wrinkled hand. As Boone felt her being pulled from his side, he yelled to Wayne, "Do you have her?"

"She's safe Boone!" Noel assured him. "It's your turn."

Wayne's hand was close, but he now understood Kaylee's hesitation. He had to let go of what made him feel safe. He reached out his hand, but the tips of Wayne's finger were not close enough. "I can't reach you!"

"Try again!" Wayne called. Boone leaned in as far as he could, then he felt Wayne's hand. He tried to grasp it, but he wasn't able to get a good grip. His hands were wet and slippery. "Let go, I've got you!"

Longing to be out of the cold water, Boone closed his eyes and held his breath. He knew he had to have faith, just as he had asked his sister to do. Before he could come up with another plan, he thrust his body towards the water's edge and grasped

Wayne with his other hand. Boone held tight, trusting his friend to pull him to safety.

Hoisted up from the ice bath he had not meant to take, Boone welcomed the cold, solid ground beneath him. Wayne was stretched out on the hard cave floor. Noel sat beside Kaylee rubbing her arms to warm her, and wringing the water from her dripping hair and dress. Boone tried to stand up and squeeze the water from his own clothes, but his leg buckled with the weakness of his ankle. Case came up beside him and handed him the plaid button up shirt he had put on that morning. "Here, I had a t-shirt on underneath."

Boone took the generosity, peeled off his dripping shirt and put on the dry one. Wayne followed Case's lead and did the same with his top layer. The boys turned their back as Noel helped Kaylee out of her drenched dress and into Wayne's shirt. The cotton long sleeve shirt was lengthy on her, but she welcomed the warm dry cloth. "I think you're going to start a new fashion trend," he said to Kaylee, knowing that would cheer her up.

"Guys," Case called with a fading flashlight in hand. "I think we are losing this one." The beam coming from his flashlight had grown much dimmer.

"We should probably keep moving," Boone suggested. He still felt groggy, but didn't know what else they could do. Case helped Boone to his feet.

Tired and sluggish, the rest stood up wearily and continued their journey between the rivers that were now much wider than when they had first started on their quest. Time passed slowly for the travelers; minutes seemed like hours and hours seemed like days. They had no idea how far they had gone or how long they had been down below their home.

Boone hobbled along barefooted since his shoes had been swept upriver. His exposed toes were the first to feel the sharp formations changing the terrain under their feet. Above him cone-like structures grew like daggers from the ceiling. "Stalagmites and stalactites," he remembered from fourth grade science. He was always confused as to which one went up and which one hung down.

"We can't go on!" Noel yelled back from the front of the group. Up ahead their light exposed a field of rock formations opening like a mouth of giant teeth ready to devour anyone of them that entered.

"We can climb through them!" Boone called up to her, wondering what the big deal was.

"No, look!" she pointed on each side of them. The rivers were diverging into two completely separate directions. "We have to choose."

"Which way takes us home, Bubby?" Kaylee asked stopping to look back at her brother.

"I don't know." He didn't want to make the decision. The group was down to one flashlight, which he now held. He shined it all around hoping to find something, anything that would tell them the way. He moaned. Not only was he frustrated and angry, but the intensity of pain running through his body was growing. They were all looking at him to point the way. "I guess we look around? Maybe there is a marker or something that can show us the way. The symbol back at the tomb led us out, so there has to be something to lead us in the right direction. Right?"

"Unless whoever built the tomb already knew the way out," Wayne suggested.

"Don't be so negative!" Noel snarled.

"What? I'm just saying," he shrugged.

"Everyone, start looking!"

The five searched every rock, looking from top to bottom in what insufficient light their one flashlight provided. Feeling blindly around the cave structures, Case wandered off by himself. "Over here! This way!" he called to the others. "Let me see that!" he said removing the light from Boone's hand. Case led them into the sharpness of the cave's mouth. He pointed to a wide column at its center. "I found this!" Carved into the massive limestone cylinder was another symbol, a harp.

"It's right in the middle. It doesn't tell us which way to go," Wayne pointed out.

"It's something," Case replied sarcastically.

"He's right," Noel interjected. "So far, each of these symbols has given us a clue." Hoping it would be similar to the one they had found previously, she scratched at it with her fingernail and then frowned.

"Okay then," Boone said. "Maybe it's another Bible reference."

"Angels play harps!" Kaylee said with excitement.

"Maybe, but I don't think that's it," Boone said gently letting her down.

"David played the harp," Case said shyly. Everyone stared at him surprised. "What?" he questioned. "It has to do with music, doesn't it?"

"I missed that one too," Wayne recalled. "Who's David?"

"Alright, Case, what else do you know?" Noel asked him.

"So, we all know the story of David and Goliath, don't we?" Case asked. He was positive that everyone, including Wayne, would know that story.

"Oh…that David," Wayne said.

"Yah, that David. Well, that same David was pretty good at playing the harp. Story goes that he would play his harp to sooth the king from evil spirits or bad dreams or something. When David played, they went away. King Saul *really* liked David. He kept him around for a while until he became jealous of him and tried to have him killed. Later, David would become king of the Israelites."

"Great! So all we need to do is play the harp, this evil looking cavern goes away, and we are shown the way out. Perfect!" Boone said weakly. "Who knows how to play the harp?" Since there were no harp players, he continued to look around the magnificent feature for more answers or perhaps some ancient instructions on harp playing.

"David was a king!" Noel jumped in. "It's not about the harp. It's what the harp *led* him to become. We need something that has to do with a king! That will *lead* us out!"

"Would a crown do?" Boone asked pointing to the opposite side of the grand column. He had discovered another symbol.

"This is amazing!" Noel said clasping her hands together in admiration. "Look at the points on the crown!" On five points of the crown, five stones had been placed. Four were a different shade of shimmery quartz rock: pale pink, milky white, light lavender and a dark purple. The fifth was plain and ordinary as if it had been picked up from the cave ground.

"You're right," he said examining the symbol suspiciously. "Noel! I think you are on to something! David picked up five smooth stones, but he only threw one of them!" He reached out for the image and began prying out the brightest and most sparkling of the five stones with his fingers.

"Wait!" Case yelled pushing Boone's hand away from the pillar. "I haven't told you the rest."

"You know more? And I thought you came for the doughnuts," Wayne poked at him.

"Whatever," Case joked back. "I know that this man took his music seriously, you know, like me. I might have studied him…some."

"So, when are you going to start killing giants?" Noel laughed at her own joke. Not stirring a response from him, she cleared her throat. "Okay, so what else?"

"If you are all done," he said acting as serious as he knew how, "there's a part of the story after David was king when that guy kind of dropped dead…"

"What? Did some guy die because he touched his crown?" Boone asked feeling distressed.

"No, not the crown, it was something else," Noel cut in. "When David tried to move the Ark of the Covenant into Jerusalem, you know, the big box that held the Ten Commandments and a bunch of other stuff, he didn't do it right.

He had it brought in on a cart, which was not how God had instructed it to be moved in the first place. God was specific about those things. The animals pulling the cart got spooked and the ark almost fell. A man named Uzzah reached out for it, touched the Ark of the Covenant and the Lord took him out right there for his irreverence."

"But all the guy tried to do was catch it!" Wayne said angrily.

"Maybe," she answered, "but it doesn't matter. God told them not to touch it. He had specific instructions for how to carry it and David hadn't done it right."

"So, you're saying that either we pick the right one or we die. Okay, no pressure. Any ideas?"

"I have a theory," Noel suggested. "David *only* threw one, so which one?" The others waited patiently nervous for Noel. "It's this one!" She reached her hand up to the crown and removed the center stone. The entire group gasped. Everyone looked around in confusion as if the hard floor was going to give way burying them deeper in the earth.

"What were you thinking?" Case shouted, once he realized that she had actually chosen correctly. "How did you know which one to choose?"

"David might have been a king, but he had to kill the giant first. The Bible said he threw a stone," she smiled, holding up the ordinary rock she had removed from the symbol.

"You're right! He threw it," Boone agreed, accidentally bringing the attention back to him. "David didn't hold on to the stone. He slung it. That one throw at the giant gave him the direction for the rest of his life." The travelers followed Boone's gaze to the roof of the giant's mouth. Naturally formed on the cave ceiling and illuminated by their remaining light was the six point Star of David.

"Boone, would you do the honor?" Noel requested, handing the stone to him.

"No thanks. I… um…" Boone stuttered. He didn't want to tell her that he was afraid he would miss. "Here Case, you do it."

Case took the stone, focused on his target, leaned back, and tossed it to the center of the star where it stuck tight. At first, the room was still, but then tiny stones began to rain down on them. The ceiling above them started to shake. Frightened and anticipating another cave in, the group ducked down covering their heads. The light shaking increased to a violent jolt. The quake dislodged the large column beside them from its home and slammed it down into the river to their right. A wave of water billowed over and drenched the five travelers.

Once again soaking wet, Boone shined his light on the pillar, he saw that it created a bridge across the river to a narrow path along its side.

"Awesome!" Wayne held his hand up for a high five.

Boone did the same. "Lead the way!" Boone motioned to his cousin, Case.

"No thanks. This is your gig," he replied.

"Really," Boone insisted.

"Alright! Seeing as how I'm *awesome*, I should be the one!" Case bragged stepping onto the collapsed formation. Boone handed him the flashlight as he motioned for the drenched and cold group to follow him. The group hesitantly climbed up behind him and proceeded across.

"Hold my hand, Boone," Kaylee said nervously. He grabbed her hand and held it tightly.

"Let's go!" Case called back to them. Boone had never seen this side of Case before. He couldn't decided if he would like this new take charge Case, but at least now, the others wouldn't look to him as someone to follow.

Chapter 12

With Case in the lead, Boone followed behind the group. Their bodies were sluggish from fatigue and hunger; they moved slower now. The walls of the cave were becoming even more jagged and uncomfortable to rest against. The group found themselves climbing over rock formations and under low hanging stalactites in order to stay with the river running beside them.

Wayne had Kaylee on his back. Her eyes were closed and Boone guessed she would be asleep in a matter of minutes. He felt sorry for her - sorry that he had gotten her into this hole of a mess. He remembered the excitement he and Noel had enjoyed that night in the attic when they found the red leather book and how at that moment there had been no disagreement between them and they were still best friends. She said they were good, but Boone wondered if things would change once they got back, if they ever got back. He remembered the church windows, the voices, and the library. He recalled the hope of a fairy tale city and the fortune within. Now for the first time, he realized that he hated those books and most of all he still hated Elijah Craig.

His ankle was hurting, the pain intensifying with every step. He had to stop and rest. As he sank to the ground, Noel leaned over him to investigate the wound on his face. "I think it might be infected. That could explain the fever. Can you go on?" Boone was still feeling nauseous. Noel was right. He did have a fever.

"Sure," he answered untruthfully.

"Why don't you get the guys to help you? I can carry Kaylee."

He didn't want to tell her the truth. He needed help, but he didn't want anyone to have to carry him. "I can do it on my own. Thanks anyway."

"Okay, I was only trying to help," she halfway shrugged.

Boone looked around to assess the situation. It wasn't good. The path beside the river had narrowed. They were now clinging to the walls to keep from being swept into the fast-moving water that was getting rougher, almost rapid like. He rested his arm on the wall to hold his body up. Something soft brushed against his palm. Looking closer, he saw a strange green substance. They had traveled into an area of the cave where sporadic patches of moss were oddly growing through cracks onto the damp cave walls.

"Hey, over here! Quick!" Wayne's voice barely echoed in the cavern over the sound of the rushing water, it was enough to distract Boone from his discovery. "Over here!" Wayne yelled louder. Noel ran towards the other three with Boone limping slowly behind. "Check it out!"

"It's glowing!" Case shouted. In front of them, the swiftly moving water appeared to have a subtle glow.

"It's not glowing!" Boone announced excitedly. "It's light! There must be light up ahead to make the water look brighter! It has to be the way out!" A sudden burst of excitement woke the travelers from their slump; even Kaylee was alert and ready to go forward.

"Perfect timing," Noel commented shaking the last bit of battery life out of her flashlight.

The five picked up their pace, determined to reach the point at which the light was making the water glow. The further they went, the brighter the water grew and the steeper the ledge on which they had been traveling became. The growth on the walls grew thicker with roots emerging on the cave ceiling above them. Understanding that they must not be far from the surface, hope filled them. The realization that they were closer to home started to sink in. Knowing that soon they would be above ground, they joked carelessly with each other. However, the faster they moved and the brighter the water, the tighter the cave wall became. Soon, they were walking single file on a narrow piece of rock. Their joy abruptly ceased when they recognized that they could go no further.

Directly in front of them was a wall of stone, covered with vines and patches of moss. "I don't get it," Boone shivered looking at the water ten feet or so down in the canyon beside them. "I thought this would lead us out." The cave had closed in around them except for an opening at the bottom. The river itself would have been halted as well, but the opening allowed the water to flow underneath it.

"Me too," Noel said exposing her disappointment.

"What do we do, Bubby?" Kaylee whined.

"Look around," Noel jumped into the conversation. "Every time we've been stuck, we've always had a clue or a symbol telling us where to go next. There has to be another one."

"Say we do find a symbol again," Case proposed, "how can we trust whoever put them here? We were supposed to be looking for some bride. Now, we're stuck in a dumb cave. I say we sit here and let someone find us."

"Who's going to find us, Case?" Boone asked calmly.

"Don't know, Boone," Case snapped back at Boone. "Why don't you and your girlfriend tell us, since you got us into this mess!'

"She's not my girlfriend!" Boone yelled back sharply.

"That's right! She's your *best* friend…what Wayne and I used to be. Seriously, this whole thing is your fault," Case jeered pointing his finger at Boone.

"Hey guys, stop," Wayne interrupted. "If it's anyone's fault, let's try Miss I Know Everything Even How To Turn My Hair Pink."

"What!" Noel huffed, "It was supposed to be fun, not dangerous. If you all would have listened to me, we wouldn't even be here!"

"I said we should wait, but…"

"Boone," Kaylee's soft voice calmed the feud and stopped Noel, "look at the pretty flowers."

The teen's eyes followed Kaylee's pointed finger to the imprinted symbols of three flowers on the wall above the river tunnel.

Noel beamed with satisfaction. Looking directly at Case, she mocked, "Told you." The furthest of the symbols was a flower with five petals. The second, looked like lilies, a grouping of five blooming flowers growing together. On the right and closest to the teens, the third was a single flower, one that had not yet bloomed, closed up tight in its petals.

"All right, we have to think," Boone told everyone over the rush of the water. "So far, all of our clues have come from the Bible. Chances are, so will this one." The mood changed instantly. Putting aside their anger, they all grew silent trying to recall Bible verses they had memorized in their early years of Sunday school, or hoping to remember a sermon that could help them decipher this riddle.

A familiar excitement took over inside of Boone, like it had overtaken him a week ago when he and Noel had shuffled through the attic books. "*You are him that worketh not,*" the voice echoed around him. "*You are him,*" it called to him louder. The anxiousness returned. Last Sunday, they were all sitting together in church when the red glow had fallen on the pages of his Bible, and he had the vision of he and Noel working in a garden.

"The garden," Boone shouted to the others. "The garden of Eden, Adam and Eve! God gave them a garden to live in." The others stared at him as if he hadn't spoken to them before. "Noel, grab your Bible. Genesis has the story of the creation," he screamed over the roar and splash of the underground river. Noel slung her backpack off her shoulders and reached inside.

"Boone! It's gone!"

"What do you mean it's gone?" he questioned.

"I mean, it's not in here. It's gone," she almost cried. "I must have dropped it somewhere."

"Great," Wayne mumbled, sliding down the bumpy cave wall to dangle his feet over the edge. "Now what?"

"Like *I* said," Case said sitting down beside Wayne, "we wait."

"Let's think. We all know the creation story," Noel stated. She tossed her backpack on her shoulders while keeping her balance on the narrow walkway.

"But it has to be a specific scripture. All the symbols have led us to exact scriptures or passages," Boone replied.

Kaylee blankly stared at the cave wall appearing unaware of the conversation behind her. Her soft still voice again silenced the feuding friends, "The Lord God planted a garden toward the east in Eden; and there He placed a man whom He had formed."

"What was that, sis?" Boone asked inching over to her side.

"It's my Bible verse Bubby," she answered smiling up at him.

"That's great, Kaylee," Boone said hugging her. "That's great!"

"God planted a garden . . . " Noel repeated. "B, how do you plant something?"

He looked at her confused. "With your hands?"

"Exactly!"

He knew that she was on to something. "But how are we going to get your hands all the way over there," he asked.

"Not me Boone, you."

"Why me?" Boone stepped back unwillingly.

"Because you're him!" Wayne said sarcastically. Case burst into hysterics.

"Very funny guys," Boone responded. "Say I do it. How do you expect me to get up there? Walk on water?"

"Well, I was actually thinking you could jump," Noel suggested doubtfully.

"Jump? The river has to be at least twenty feet across. If I fall, I'm going to get sucked under that cave wall and then who knows what will happen."

"But if you do make it, we might all get out of here," Noel replied.

"What was that?" Case shouted brushing frantically at his head.

"What was what?" Boone asked.

"That thing that landed on my head!"

"There's nothing on your head, Case," Noel said checking her own head for any unwanted visitors.

Boone did the same and hastily surveyed their surroundings. It was then that he found what had startled Case. A network of long thick dangling roots had forced themselves through the stone. "There's your mystery something," Boone said relieved. Now it occurred to him exactly how he was going to get across.

His uneasiness turned into a calm certainty. He glanced down at the glowing water and then up at the wall with the three symbols. "It's like the ropes in gym class," he rationalized. "I have to touch one of the three flowers." Kaylee had recited that the garden was in the east. So he would go with the one closest to them and hope for the best.

"Swing back, Boone," Case tried to encourage. "When you hit the wall, swing back hard and we will get you."

It sounded like a good idea. "Swing back," he reminded himself. Boone was sure that Elijah Craig would not have done this, at one time there had to be another way. There wasn't much room to get a good run in before the jump. He backed as close as he could to the rough cave wall, gripped a longer root, and gave it a hard tug. He breathed in deeply and looked at Noel. She had her head bowed, eyes closed, and appeared to be deep in prayer. "That's a good idea," he thought. "Lord, don't let me die." Boone meant it. He wasn't ready to die.

The roar of the water crashing on the wall in front of them was deafening. Boone's ankle pulsated. He reached down to touch the swollen joint, and then he took four quick steps and leapt.

His hand successfully smacked the first flower at its center, at first nothing happened. Boone felt for a minute that time was standing still, but then his body began to fall. The symbol began to move, pulling itself back into the wall. His hands slipped down more. *Swing back*, he reminded himself, but he couldn't move his body. The more he wiggled to get the vine to move, the further he slipped down. He held it tight. The root started to loosen its grip on the cave ceiling. His friends were terror stricken as the vine released itself from its hold on the earth above. He expected to sink into the water below him, but instead he landed with an insignificant splash on something slick and hard. He stood up awkwardly amid the illuminated waters. The river was very shallow on the rock, but still moving fast. He tried to balance, but his ankle gave in sending him to his knees. The water splashed heavily into his face.

"Reach for my hand," Wayne shouted. Boone extended his arm, but this time he couldn't reach Wayne's long arm.

"Can you jump back?" Noel shouted doubtful in her question. He shook his head. The pain was searing. He tried to stand, but slipped again. He went down, this time on his chest. A clap of thunder shook the cavern and vibrated the walls surrounding him. Boone tried to hold on to the rock formation below him. The screams of his friends echoed around him as he desperately clung to the rock. He strained to look over, but the water was dragging him to where it was escaping. He gulped, pulling in a mouthful of the icy cave water. Gasping for air, water filled his mouth. His fingers were beginning to lose their grip.

Frantically, he tried to dig them in deeper. The thunder grew louder, drowning out the screaming of the others. The water overtook Boone's shoulders, his neck, and finally his head. He tried with all his might to swim back, but the current was too strong. He couldn't help but wonder if this was the end, if his prayer had not been heard and he would die. The beating of his heart slowed down. Then, he could feel no more.

Chapter 13

Boone felt the coolness of the soft cotton pillow on his cheek as he rolled to his side. He pulled the sheets up under his neck and tried to settle back to sleep. "What a nightmare," he moaned. "Crashing windows, stupid symbols, glowing water…" He breathed in heavily hoping to inhale the smell of his mom's cheesy scrambled eggs and homemade wheat bread, but the smell was different. It was clean and grassy, like being outside in early June. Boone tried to roll back, but a dull pain on the side of his head encouraged him to stay right where he was. He reached up and rubbed the gauzy covering that had been placed on his wound. "It wasn't a dream," he murmured. He touched the bandage again and tried to think through his memories. "We must have been rescued. We made it to the spring," he chuckled. "I did it! I really did it!"

He snuggled back into the fresh sheets. They were warm, like how his clothes felt when they had immediately come out of the dryer. He drew them closer to his nose hoping to inhale the clean combination of laundry detergent and fabric softener, but instead his nose filled with the flowery scent of lavender. "These aren't my sheets! Where am I?" Boone shouted sitting straight up in bed. Then, it dawned on him. "Where's Kaylee, and Noel, the guys?" With his sudden movement, the pain spread rapidly across his bones, his head wound pounded.

Boone opened his eyes to blinding light. He closed them tightly and then cautiously undid his eyelids one at a time, allowing the brightness to seep in and his pupils to adjust. All around him he saw white. The room he was in was like a giant igloo made of white stone. The dome shape loomed above his head like a beehive with a circular opening in the top to allow the light to pour through. His bed was simple and covered completely in white linens. Beside his bed sat a wooden chair and a table adorned with a vase of bright orange flowers. The walls were bare with not even a picture or a window. Across from his bed was a door-like opening, blocked by a sheer white cloth. "Where am I?" he asked himself again. A soft wind swept into the room accompanied by a hint of mint. Intrigued, Boone breathed it in thinking it smelled like chewing gum. He tried to move again, but his body was weary and drained.

"You're all right!" Wayne shouted pushing the cloth doorway aside and rushing to Boone's bedside. "No fair! Your room is twice the size of ours and we have to share. You had us all stressed out."

Case entered a little slower with his head down. He couldn't look Boone in the eye. "You woke up, that's good. Um, listen; about all that stuff I said before, back in the cave, I'm real sorry. I shouldn't have said those things. Then when we thought you were gone…"

Boone didn't know how to respond to him, so he glanced over at Wayne for support. Like Case, he was not dressed in his normal tattered blue jeans and untucked t-shirt. Instead they each wore overalls made of a pale tan cloth that hung loose, but tidy on their frames. Neither of them were at all surprised that they were standing in the bleached rock room.

"What's going on?" Boone asked feeling weary. "Where am . . . " His inquiry was cut off by a voice with a thick southern accent.

"Out ya go, boys. Back to the garden with you," the voice of a short, but rather large elderly woman bellowed. Her hair was stark white and pulled tightly into a bun on top her head. Her skin was clear and free of any wrinkles. She wore a long dress that was similar in color to the tan worn by his friends. A white apron draped neatly over her front. In her hands she held a wooden platter displaying containers of varying sizes and a single wooden cup. "It's my time now."

"See you later, Boone." Wayne waved to his bed-ridden friend as he and Case started to leave.

"Wait," Boone called to them. "Kaylee and Noel?"

The boys were quickly out the door before they had heard him. The woman set the tray on the table beside Boone, placed her hand on his forehead for a few seconds, examined his eyes, and then oddly checked his teeth and fingernails. "Fever's gone. The girls are with the gardener now. They just fine," she smiled tightly with her eyes squinting cheerfully. "You got a nasty bump there, Leader. I can fix you right up. You let old Aggie take care of ya. Umm, Ummm, He is so good. You should've been dead after that dive you took. You young ones are so blessed to find us you know. Oh yes, amazing are the things He does here. You'll see, Leader."

"I'm sorry," Boone interrupted her nonsensical talking. "Where am I? Who's he and why do you keep calling me Leader?"

Aggie chuckled as she lifted and opened one of the tiny bottles on the tray. "You're in our Mishpachah, Leader."

"No, no, no...this isn't real. It's a story, a fairy tale. It's not real. It's a dream. We were rescued, but now, I'm lying in a hospital bed with people all around begging me to wake up. That's it!" Boone lay his head back down slowly on the pillow and closed his eyes. He was so exhausted that he could barely discern what was happening. This was a dream. He was certain of it.

Maybe if he kept his eyes closed he would wake up in his real bed, with his real sheets, in his real room.

Aggie lifted the bandage off his head. Boone winced at his very real pain. A cool sensation came over him as she carefully smeared the contents of the vile on his wound. It tingled and calmed the sting. "Aloe is good for a lot of things, Leader, including burns. It will sure make a good bump feel a lot better. Here, drink this. It's good for the insides." Boone lifted his head off of the pillow, blindly trusting this strange woman. He guessed that if she were going to hurt him, she wouldn't have gone to so much trouble to care for him this far. She lifted the wooden cup to his lips. Honey. He tasted the honey. "It's chamomile tea with a hint of bee pollen. It's my own blend. It will calm ya down a bit and help ya to sleep."

Her face was pleasant and peaceful. "Thank you," he managed to say. Boone still wasn't sure what to think or what to believe.

"You're welcome, Leader. You lay back. It's good for us all to rest, especially when we're healing. Oh, even us healers gets to rest when it's our time. The gardener will be in when you're ready. My job is done for now." She placed the cup back on the tray and exited through the opening in the room. The taste of the sweet chamomile tea lingered in his mouth. He pulled the sheets back up around him and drifted unintentionally off to sleep.

Boone was unaware of how much time had passed when he woke up. A warm breeze slipped through the doorway, bringing with it the smells of flowers, mint, and ripening fruit. This time, he opened his eyes to find an elderly man looking over him watchfully. His eyes were a light blue and his skin was dark and smooth. On his head, he wore a hat woven of straw. A few strands of silver white hair peeped from under the brim. He wore the same overalls that Case and Wayne had been wearing with a loose white shirt underneath covering his arms. On the breast of the bibbed pants embroidered in gold thread was the beehive. The man's hands were clasped in his lap as if he had been praying.

A smile grew on the person beside him. "Son," the stern voice began, "I'm the gardener and you can just call me that for now." Boone opened his mouth to speak, but had no idea what he was going to say. "Questions? I knew you would have them. I won't have all the answers, but I can usually help folks find them. Sometimes, I let folks figure them out for themselves," he said with a wink. Boone opened his mouth to talk, but the words wouldn't come out. "It's all right, son. Go ahead."

"I know you, don't I?" Boone asked. He was sure he had seen this man many times.

"I should say you do by now. We'll talk about that later."

"But, where am I? Am I dead?" Boone was really starting to wonder. "Are you…are you God? Is this Heaven?"

The old man chuckled, "Oh no, far from it. Like I told ya before, I'm the gardener. This garden ain't gonna grow itself. However, a lot of people wish it would. It's always growing; it's working to produce the fruit. People are like gardens. No fruit, no garden. Like the gardeners that have come before me, I protect it, make sure we're doing things the way they supposed to be done, and show people how to do what they can do best." Boone stared at him. "Guess I really didn't answer your questions, now did I, son? How 'bout I show you around? Let me step out and get some people to help lift you up."

Boone slowly sat up in the bed, swung his legs around, and placed his feet on the wood planked floor below him. He was eager to see what was outside the walls of his room. He had to find out if this really was the magical place of his childhood tales. He discovered that his ankle no longer throbbed and his feet no longer carried cave mud on them. "No thanks," he said. "I can do it myself." He stood up and then fell back down on the cotton sheets.

"Son, one thing you'll learn about this place is when one goes down, we lift um up. And son, you went down hard." He walked to the door and motioned with a wave of his arm for others to come inside. The entrance of four people followed the gardener's motioning. They each were dressed in garments of the same hand spun cotton, but each one wore a different symbol on their chest. The first to enter was a girl not much older than Boone. Her hair was red and her cheeks lightly freckled. On her dress was embroidered a pod of grapes.

Behind her were two men, twins, dressed in the same cotton work overalls. "Hello," they addressed him in unison, smiling the same tooth filled smile. They walked the same, sounded the same, and even tipped their straw hats the same, but their symbols were very different. The first wore a harp, like the one they had seen in the cave. The second wore a boat like the one he and Noel had seen on the floor of the storeroom. To Boone's surprise, a little girl entered last. *You've got to be kidding,* he thought. *She's a child.* Her brown eyes caught Boone's concerned gaze. She ran to the gardener and hugged him tightly. He returned the gentle squeeze.

"Look, Leader," her soft voice directed to Boone. "I'm a leader like you, at least one day I will be." She stepped to his side and pointed at the tree of life that was sewn into his clothing.

Boone glanced down. For the first time, he realized that he was not in his own clothes. He traced over the golden threads with the tips of his fingers. The stitches were tiny and delicate, as if they were done by hand. He too wore the bibbed overalls worn by the other men around him. He looked to the gardener to question the where about of his shoes, but before he could get a word out, four pair of hands were lifting him to his feet and guiding him steadily to the opening.

The gardener pulled back the sheer white cloth as Boone was carried out. He raised his arms high in the air and cheerfully shouted, "Welcome to the Mishpachah!

Chapter 14

"We're still in the cave!" Boone exclaimed. The lifters carefully lowered him to his feet and left the gardener alone to steady Boone for his first look at the Mishpachah. It was more breathtaking than he had ever imagined and bigger than any of the stories he had heard as a child. "How is this possible?" Boone was so taken by all that he saw that the words spewed from his mouth before he could process them. "I don't believe what I'm seeing! Are those coconuts? It's like a jungle, no wait, a farm, or a garden!"

Boone wished that Noel were here with him; she would be fascinated and have a million questions. Then it occurred to him that he didn't know where she was. The air around him was warm and comfortable and a big change from the cave they had coincidentally discovered. The smell of orange blossoms danced past him in the breeze.

The gardener stood by Boone on the great rock ledge that overlooked the neatly organized rows of plants, vines, and orchards that helped to create the world below. To his right were the nut bearing trees growing as magnificent in height as they were in number. Others in the fruit forest flowered with red blossoms and pink leaves. Most of which he had never seen before. It was the most unique forest he had ever laid eyes on. Beyond the trees Boone saw fields of grains, and to his left, crops of vegetables, and beyond that, the fruits of the vine eagerly climbing up their trellises. Directly below him, the earth granted herbs and spices that wildly blanketed the area like a colorful quilt intentionally seasoning the growth around them. The aroma rising up formed a concoction of spice and comfort that was better than any perfume or fragrance Boone had ever smelled.

Among the rows were hundreds of people. All were busy about their trade planting and preparing. A few picked up the fruit that had fallen to the ground, while others sat with groups of children under the trees. Behind Boone was his room, one dome among many. At the center of the stone igloos, a marble structure emerged like a giant beehive watching over the ones below. Moving in and out, the workers carried the fruits of the garden to the place where they would best be used.

Boone watched as workers toting large wicker baskets full of apples passed by others holding stacks of neatly pressed blankets and pillows. A lady with her arms full of newly sewed work clothing nodded her head at Boone with a smile. Wondering if she had made his clothes as well, Boone smiled back. No one he saw moved too fast or too slow. They moved contentedly, happily living their lives apart from his world. Warm smells of freshly baked bread emerged from another dome. It reminded him of home, and that he was extremely hungry. Boone turned back to observe the wonders below and then gazed at the cave ceiling realizing that there was no sun or gigantic chandelier to provide light.

The gardener noticed Boone's confusion. "The mist provides the light, Leader." Directly in front of him and behind the acres of growth, two waterfalls crashed into two rivers. The clear water circled around an island of land isolated from the rest of the garden. The rivers then joined and flowed into one large river that ran through its center. From the river, a mist billowed up and spread throughout the entire place creating a white veil throughout the cave, filling it with light and moisture. "Is this for real?" he finally was able to ask the gardener.

The gardener chuckled and pointed to the top of the waterfall. "I'd say so, Leader. I've been here a very long time. I know getting here was difficult, but you can rest now. You've shaken things up around here. We don't have many visitors come in the way you did."

"We weren't trying to visit," Boone corrected.

"Oh, is that so?"

"We were looking for," he stopped hesitant as to whether or not he should go on.

"What were you looking for, Leader?" the gardener questioned, carefully studying Boone for an answer.

"I don't know, something childish. We got lost."

"Most people who are looking are usually lost in some way, Leader. Maybe we can help you find what you're looking for," the gardener offered sympathetically.

The gardener's awkward wording and unclear statements were not a consolation to Boone. "Can you help me find my sister, and the others?"

"They're fine; doing their jobs until it's time for someone else to do it for them." Boone began to feel overwhelmed by the newness of his condition. He wanted so much for the strange voice that had followed him around the past couple of days to confirm that this was where he was supposed to be. He wanted something familiar, something to tell him everything was going to be okay.

The gardener led Boone across the middle of seven suspended bridges and to a rock pillar that towered slightly to the left of the main river. The connecting bridges, and the spiral staircase carved into the support, provided access between the domes and land below. "We use everything that we work to grow for our survival," the gardener pointed out as they descended to the base of the Mishpachah. As they walked, the gardener stayed close by Boone's side. Then he stopped, bent down, and picked up a hard-shelled pod. He pulled back the rough edges and removed from it a soft white fiber. "Cotton," he smiled. "You're wearing it."

The gardener showed Boone everything from lavender and rosemary to tomatoes and broccoli. In each well-designed row the gardener showed him, workers stopped what they were doing to talk with the gardener, or give a friendly wave. As a child, Boone had imagined that the people in the Mishpachah would be shorter, maybe blue, have wings, and talk in really high-pitched voices. He never imagined them as real people.

Boone had once dreamed of finding this place of urban legend, but now, he struggled to determine whether or not he was actually in awe or possibly afraid. The garden was a far reach from the concrete walls of school, and despite the appearance of what he saw as normal people, Boone felt like he was in an over the top science experiment. It wasn't ordinary, and he wasn't sure if he could stay here long enough to accept it.

They were continuing on their walk, the gardener talking and Boone trying to listen when a loud buzz came too close to his ear. He swatted at the tiny creature, but missed contact with it when the little leader who had been secretly following them shouted, "NO!"

"It's okay, child," the gardener soothed the teary eyed girl. "He doesn't know."

"He could have killed it!" she cried.

"Leader, they won't hurt you. Where there are bees, there is life," the gardener assured him.

The whole place was swarming with tiny honeybees, but no one seemed to be bothered by them or fearful that they might be stung. Their buzzing joined in with the sweet songs that were being sung by all throughout the garden. It reminded Boone of the stained glass windows, his science class daydream, and the swarm of bees that they had encountered under the cemetery. The gardener led him to the point at the river's edge where the two streams merged into one. "It's good to drink the water,

Leader. It will refresh you." The gardener bent down holding his hat on with one hand and took a sip with the other.

Boone started to do the same, but the minty scent was stronger than it had been in his room. He breathed in deeply. The smell of mint masked the divine fragrance of the garden and overpowered his senses. It entered his brain, making him feel disoriented and woozy. He dropped to his knees confident that he was going to throw up.

Immediately, the hands of those who had been nearby were lifting him gently to his feet. "Let them help you. It can be overwhelming at first to new workers. You'll get used to it's being after awhile, but you can't ignore that it's here," the gardener encouraged.

"Awhile? You mean like a few days? I don't know. This place, it's unbelievable, but we can't stay. We have to get home."

"You don't need to worry about time. This is your home Leader, until you are ready to go."

"I'm sorry. This is really great and all, but there's some kind of mistake. I'm not Leader. I'm just Boone. Our being here was an accident, that's all." He was beginning to feel very out of place.

The gardener pointed to a distant figure in a patch of bright orange pumpkins. Boone watched as Wayne happily carried water to another worker. The worker talked to Wayne for a moment and then looked over in the direction of Boone.

"Hey!" Wayne shouted excitedly waving in Boone's direction. He said a couple of words to the person tending to the pumpkins and then ran towards him. "It's about time you got out of bed. There's work to be done!"

"Wayne, it's me, Boone," he leaned in. "Don't worry, I'm starting to think this is a dream. I'll probably wake up any minute in Sunday school during the middle of one of Reed's lessons and have a great story to tell you after church, right?" He studied Wayne's eyeballs for a sign that maybe they had all been drugged or something. "Please tell me I'm right!"

Wayne laughed hard. "No drugs, no dream, and we're definitely not in Sunday school. Do you think I'd be this awake in Sunday school? It's real! You and smarty pants, I mean Observer, sorry Gardener…"

The gardener grinned. "It's all right, Timer."

"You were right! This is it!" Wayne said with more enthusiasm than Boone had ever seen from him.

Boone pulled Wayne down close to him and whispered, "If this isn't a dream, then you need to know that they're holding us hostage. This gardener person said I couldn't go home, but don't worry. I'm going to get us home."

"He probably said it's not time yet, or something like that. Everything has a time, like the dirt. Oh, wow! I just figured out why I am a timer. I know when we're supposed to plant all this stuff!"

Boone waited for Wayne to crack a joke, or disappear, or something else wacky that would happen in a dream. But he didn't. "All right, I've had enough," Boone shouted louder than he had intended, drawing the attention of the workers around him. "I want to go home. I want my house, my bed, and my clothes. I'm going to get my sister and we're going home. I don't know who or what you people think you are."

"We are the Mishpachah, Leader, and your being here is no accident, son. There is a plan for you," the gardener explained softly.

"A plan? What plan? My parents will be worried and I have an essay due by 8th period on Friday!" Boone could feel tears forming in his eyes. He hadn't cried in a long time, but he was starting to become scared of this place that had taken his friend and turned him into a blissful overalls wearing garden gnome. It wasn't normal. This was different; they were different. His life before Elijah Craig was just fine, now it was upside down.

The gardener turned to Boone and placed a supportive hand on each of his shoulders. "Deny yourself, son."

"What?" he asked in a hushed cry. "Deny myself? I don't have anything? Not even my own clothes!"

Wayne pointed at the symbol on Boone's bibs. "Leader, huh?" Then, he pointed to the hourglass symbol on his own cotton overalls. "Like I said, I'm a timer, and Case," he said smiling and pointing in the direction of the lime trees, "he's a musician, not like that's a surprise."

"Look closer, Leader," the gardener suggested. Each person that Case passed was humming the same tune and smiling. "It's not about the task we assign ourselves to do, it's why we're doing it and for whom we're doing it."

"What are you saying? If I work, then I can go home?"

The gardener patiently sighed at Boone. "When you yield what is already inside of you, then you will know your way, Leader."

"And I do this by leading and that denying thing you mentioned before?" Boone asked acting as if he understood.

"Yes, Leader," the gardener replied.

"And my sister, does she have an assignment too?"

"Kaylee is playing with the others. It is her place to be a child and to learn by watching. She is not unimportant, in fact it is her child-like faith that makes her very important."

"But…" Boone started and then nodded his head to the child that still had not left his side.

"Lifting another up is not working, Leader. It is a privilege."

Boone recognized that not even he, in all the oddness of the past few days, could have dreamed this up. There had to be more to it. His curiousness was interrupted by a woman's shrill scream. People from all areas of the garden were running towards the eastern stream. An elderly man ran up to the gardener out of breath and urgently explained, "Gardener, your healer, she has fallen."

"We have to go!" With Boone at his heels, the gardener rushed to where everyone in the garden was gathered, and pushed their way through to the core of the group.

Boone watched as those near him reached down to lift an elderly lady to her feet. She was drenched in water and shaking.

Her arms hung limp by her sides and her lightly grayed black hair hung back dripping. Hands all around him reached high in the air to assist the now weeping women.

"Forgive me!" the women cried. "Oh forgive me!"

"Gardener, what happened? Is she okay?" Boone asked for the first time forgetting about himself.

"She fell, but she'll make it," he said troubled.

"She's old and she fell in the river! How do you know she'll be okay?"

"She didn't fall in the river, Leader. She sought to cross it. She stopped using her abilities for the garden some time ago. We have spoken many times, but she had her own ways. All people fall, Leader. It's in their nature. She didn't scream because she was hurt, she screamed because she saw where she was going. We can be thankful, she turned back before she made it all the way."

The gardener walked to the spot where the lady had taken her first step and pointed to the unattended field that grew wildly between the two rivers. "It hasn't always been here, but started to grow when the founders first arrived long ago. We know now that we cannot use it. The smell that overwhelms you comes from the field. It's all around us. But if we concentrate on our purpose, we won't notice it and we won't fall. If too many fall in the garden, we grow weak."

"You told me you use everything that grows in the garden."

"I told you that we use everything that we *work* to grow. We don't work on that," the gardener replied.

"But what does it do? What happens if you go in to the field?" Boone's desire to go home had been replaced by the mystery of the abandoned plant.

"It doesn't matter to you yet. I suggest you not give into it, Leader," the gardener stated. Boone stared at the hint of purple that presented itself boldly in the field. The gardener continued, "You're a leader, son. You haven't realized it yet. It's the ability you've been gifted with. Every fiber in you has been designed to lead. You must now do this in the garden in order to protect it."

"Lead what, lead who?" Boone questioned.

"She'll be your helper. Let her help you," the gardener said looking back on the garden. Boone followed his gaze to Noel who was walking toward him.

The gardener started to walk away. "Wait! Gardener, you said to protect it. Protect it from what?"

He looked sternly into Boone's eyes and answered, "The wolves."

Chapter 15

Boone watched as the gardener walked away. "So, a leader. I would have never guessed it. You of all people! The guy who is so afraid of change that he freaked out when they changed the shape of the school's pizza last year? Maybe a puller, or possibly a timer like Wayne, but a leader?" Noel rambled on, "Aren't you excited, Boone? We made it! This is it! It's the Mishpachah! We found it! You found it! Isn't it wonderful?" Then she stopped, looked at her curly headed friend and hugged him tightly around the neck. "I thought, well...I was really worried about you."

He was blown away by her enthusiasm and hoped that maybe if he held on and didn't let her go, she would calm down long enough to listen to him. Sure, this was the place that they had sought after, but he felt trapped. It was different. He wasn't sure how to act, what to do, or what to say. His friends were comfortable and settled, yet he was not. "I guess. But it's not right, it's not normal." Boone lightly grabbed her by the arm and pulled her close. "N! What is going on? How long was I out? How did we get here?"

"All I know is that after you played Tarzan in the cave, everything started shaking. You went under and then you were gone. The river started to rise. We didn't know what to do, except jump in after you. Next thing we know, we're here. Kaylee was the only one who didn't get hurt. Case and Wayne only remember what happened before the river and waking up here. When I woke up in my room, I saw Kaylee sitting on a bed beside me. She's doing great! You've been out for a while, at least a week or two. I came to visit you every day in the healing room. We were really scared, but the gardener said you would heal when you were ready. We waited, and then we started working, living, and this kind of became our way."

"A week or two! Where's Kaylee? I have to let her know I'm okay!"

"She knows Boone. The whole garden celebrated when you started waking up. It's going to be hard to convince her to leave you know. She loves it here! Why wouldn't she? She gets to play out here everyday! It's like her home away from home!"

"But it's not our home," Boone spoke up. "I want to go home! All this stuff about jobs, and wolves, and this whole leader thing is making me more mental than I was before I got here. I think I'm even starting to see things."

"Boone, look at that symbol on your chest."

Boone peered down at his overalls. The golden threads of the tree brightened in the light of the mist. "I know...it's a tree."

"Boone, it's not just a tree! You have to remember! It's the same tree that was on the book we found in the library!" Noel tried to remind him. "Don't you see? We found it! It's everything the legend says it would be! This is the Mishpachah!"

He threw his arms up in the air, "That's what I keep hearing. Truth is we're stuck in a garden! I don't see any emeralds, gold, or diamond dust anywhere."

"You have to look past the actual garden, Boone. It's all here. I know it's not exactly as we were told it would be. Please, give it a chance. This place is much better than any fairy tale city could ever be. You'll see it. I know you will! Look past the garden," she said. "I want to go home too, Boone! But the symbols led us here! This is where we are supposed to be. It's where you're supposed to be."

Something inside him believed that this is where he belonged, but he wouldn't let it convince him. "Supposed to be? What about home? What about your mom and dad? Don't you miss them?" A few of the workers in the garden were starting to look up at them, but he didn't care.

"Boone, I don't know how to get home. I don't know if we'll ever get home, but the more time I have, the more I can learn. We were led here, Boone. Don't you see? We'll be led back too. I'm sure of it! Even if I have to do it myself."

He knew that he shouldn't have raised his voice to her. "I'm having a hard time believing any of this is real."

"Believe me, it's real," Noel declared. "I have to get back Boone."

"Back to where?"

"My work," she boasted touching the symbol of an open book on her dress. "I'm a keeper. There are three of us and we take turns. Someone is always in the hall at all times. If anyone in the garden needs to know something about their job, like how much water something needs or what an herb can be used for, I find the right book for them. It's really kind of fun. I get to read all day in the Keeper's Hall. I'm learning so much about this place. It's amazing! I really do have so much to tell you, but it will have to wait."

"Books? You get to read books all day? That doesn't sound like work."

Noel shrugged and smiled. "Someone has to do it."

"You tell people what they need to know?"

"Where are you going with this, Boone?"

"How do we get home, Noel? That's what *I* want to know?"

Noel sighed, "Alright, ever so often we see people leaving. It's as if the whole garden stops breathing for a short period of time, like they know someone is leaving and have to say goodbye. Some people go alone, others go in groups."

"How Noel?"

She sighed again and pointed at the pennyroyal. "A few go through there, but most kind of disappear."

"But the gardener said we don't go there. Did you see that lady?"

"I know. I haven't figured it out yet. Some people can do it, but others find themselves being lifted. We have already talked about it. Case and Wayne started looking around for another entrance the day Wayne woke up. This place might as well be its own city! They haven't had enough time to look everywhere, not with their work and all the celebrations." She stopped to see if Boone was listening. "I don't think they have been looking real hard though."

Boone was discouraged. He couldn't believe what he was hearing. Noel saw the concerned look on his face. "Boone, it's not what you think. We all want to go home, but something is keeping us here. Please, give it a try until we figure this all out."

Boone knew he wasn't going to get his way this time. "I'll try," he said to appease her.

"Good! Boone, I have to go. I'll do what I can, okay?" She didn't even let him answer, but took off toward the white dome.

"Hey Noel! The gardener mentioned something about you helping me."

"Help you do what?"

"I don't know, maybe it's in one of your books."

"How about I add that to my list? You're going to be fine, Leader."

As she skipped away past patches of cabbage and carrots and into the circular opening of grass that carpeted the ground in front of the spiral staircase, he thought that he heard her whistling. Boone was certain that he had never heard her whistle before. There was a time when he would have enjoyed taking on this new adventure with her, but now all he wanted was for it to be over.

The fragrances of the herbs in front of him were sweet and intoxicating. He studied the other side of the river where the orchards of orange, apple, and pomegranate trees grew, and then the largest portion of the garden on the other side where vegetables, nuts, cotton, and more grains grew. The rows were like brightly painted lines on a dirt canvas. Everywhere he looked barefooted workers were pulling weeds, watering the plants, pruning the trees, and harvesting the growth. Strolling musicians led the workers in joyful music that floated above and around all the growing things of the garden.

Boone had to admit that there was peace in the garden. There was no sense of anyone doing something that they did not want to do. No one was angry, afraid or looking for a way to leave, except him. His eyes took in every detail of the garden including the hundreds of beehives sprinkled throughout this new world.

"Honey," he recalled. A gurgling emptiness in his stomach told him that he was really hungry. "We should have eaten the honey." Then he remembered the water. There were carvings in the wall. He had swung out to touch them thinking that it might lead him home. He had struggled for air, reaching for something to hold on to, and then nothing. Boone stared intently at the falls that poured from the cave wall. At their base was the field of purple and green. He crept closer. The smell of mint smacked him in the face and tried to work its way into his head. *I can see how this could mess with someone*, Boone thought. *But why would the healer try to get to it if she knew what effect it would have on her? Was she looking for a way out too?* He had to talk to her. She could have the knowledge he needed to get home.

Evening fell on the garden. The mist began its descent to the ground and darkened the massive cave. Wayne, along with the other boys and men, carried long wooden tables to the grass clearing in front of the large dome where Noel worked. Boone slowly walked past the tables, keeping an eye out for the fallen lady, hoping to identify her. Then he saw his sister. Her hair had been braided and she wore a dress like the ones that the ladies in the garden wore. She was sitting with Noel and Case chatting on, not caring if they were really listening. "Kaylee!" he cried running over to give her a hug.

"Bubby!" she sweetly replied jumping up to squeeze him snugly. "Are you okay, Bubby? I missed you so much. The gardener said you were okay. I prayed for you Bubby. Are you hungry? You wouldn't eat. The healer tried, but you couldn't wake up."

Her voice had a calming effect on Boone. "Yes," he stated truthfully, realizing that the last time he had truly eaten was a donut at church and a few snacks in the cave. He sat down beside her at the table. Like his, each table was neatly draped with a white cloth and glowing with the light of beeswax candles that illuminated the feast before them. Wooden platters of fresh fruit, strawberries, blueberries, and bananas lined the tables. A plate of food with fresh steamed carrots, broccoli, and bright orange sweet potatoes was placed in front of each worker. Baskets of multi-grain rolls were passed down the rows. Everyone that sat around Boone was cheerful. They talked about their day, their harvest, and the fruit of the garden. They were joyful and full of life, exactly as they had been when he had seen them working earlier that day.

"I'm starving," Wayne said as he sat down beside Case, placed a cloth napkin neatly in his lap, and surveyed the feast that had been set before them.

"Rumor has it that rhubarb pie is for dessert," Case said giving Wayne a fist bump. Boone could not believe what he was seeing. Their actions were even more surprising to him than the Mishpachah itself! They were acting as if they were having Fava burgers and not a vegetarian buffet!

Then, the garden stood, prompting everyone else to rise to their feet, clasp hands with the person beside them, and bow their heads. Boone followed their lead.

"Our Father," the stern voice of an older musician began. In unison, every worker sang the same words after him. "We are humbled to be chosen to work the garden." With each phrase he sang, the people followed raising their voices excitedly. Boone opened one eye to see that his friends and even Kaylee were singing as well. "We are honored to serve and are most grateful to You our provider of this meal. We ask that You will continue to protect each one of us, as it is each one of us who are important to the fruit that is produced for Your glory and our provision. It is in Your name that we offer this prayer. Amen."

Then they all lifted their wooden cups and shouted, "Our Mishpachah!"

"Seriously, this is awesome," Case motioned to Wayne diving into his meal.

"No kidding!" Wayne commented with a mouth full of food.

"Would you two stop for a minute?" Boone shouted. The table grew quiet and then the workers began to eat again. Case, Wayne, Noel, and Kaylee looked up from their plates. "What are you doing?"

Wayne put down his roll. "We're eating. What do you think we're doing? And I know you have got to be ready to plow in."

"No, I mean this! This place, this food! This isn't school lunch!"

They sat quietly for a moment. Case was the first to speak up. "I woke up with a broken arm and some scrapes on my face. The healer came and then the gardener. When I first saw him, I figured he was that dead guy. You know, Elijah Craig. He's not. I asked. I was scared. Wayne was knocked out in the bed beside me and he was in bad shape. I wanted to leave. But the gardener, he kept calling me Musician. Boone, that's what I am. How'd he know that? He knew about Noel reading and Wayne working in the tobacco fields. He knows what we are good at. I like it, Boone. I like doing what I'm good at, and it helps people! I've never used my music to help people before! We know it's not home, but it's what we have right now. So enjoy it!"

Kaylee spoke up next, "Are we going to our home tonight, Bubby?" Boone couldn't tell if she wanted to go home now, or if she wondered how much longer she would be allowed to stay.

"I don't know . . . I hope so," he replied.

"It's nice here Boone, like home. Can mommy and daddy come see us?" she whimpered.

Seeing his sister confused and missing their parents confirmed what he had to do. If they all thought he was a leader, then he was going to lead. "Alright, here's the deal. Noel, keep on the books. Kaylee, you play, and if anyone says anything about home or a way out, you let me know at once. Got it? Case, you and Wayne keep on the lookout and watch for anyone coming or going. Visit every inch of the garden. Let me know if there is anything odd or strange."

"Why the rush? I like it here," Wayne asked.

Boone didn't have the words to respond, so he ignored him. "Any idea what's on the other side of the purple field?"

"No. The field is pennyroyal, Boone," Noel said in a cautioning whisper. "It's an herb. At home if it's used the wrong way or too much, it can be really harmful and even deadly. Here, it's different. No one takes care of it. It grows on its own, like a weed that we can't kill. We stay away from it because of what it can do. It causes problems."

"You mean like the woman that they carried off the other day?"

"Yes, like that. But here, you don't even have to touch it for it to be harmful. We were warned not to get too close."

"I'm so confused," Boone said burying his face in his hands, "it doesn't make sense. How can that be a way out for some, but not everyone? I can't wait to get out of here!" He looked to Wayne and then to Case. "You know what we *need* to do, right?"

Kaylee perked up to her usual sassy self. "Who put you in charge?"

Boone joined in with her amusement. "The gardener, smarty." He was still in awe at how his friends had changed. He was hungry, but somehow the veggies in front of him didn't look too appetizing. He pushed his plate aside and reached to the center of the table for a strawberry and a blueberry muffin.

"May I take your plate?" asked the youthful voice of a girl about his age.

"Sure," Boone perked up. Her gown bore the symbol of the single flower. Her hair was such a dark color of brown that it could easily have been mistaken for black.

"I know that one!"

"You might," the dark headed girl laughed, "you saw me in the cotton field today. I am an observer."

"No, your symbol. I remember your symbol." Noel glared at Boone, giving him the eye to hush what he was saying. Then it hit him. It was the last symbol he had seen in the cave and the one that had sent him down to the garden. "The garden of Eden, something about hands," he mumbled. Boone still couldn't remember everything that had happened, but he visibly remembered that symbol.

"I'm very sorry, but I do not think I can help you," she smiled, blinking her soft green eyes and putting a wave of brown hair behind her ear. "Here, let me take your plate. I am assisting in the kitchen tonight."

"Do you need help?" Boone offered. He caught a glimpse of Noel rolling her eyes.

"No thank you, Leader," she said and walked away.

"What was that about, Boone? Suddenly, you are interested in working?" Noel inquired.

"I need to talk to her. I want to know why the symbol on her dress was the one that about killed me. That's what it was about," Boone emphasized. Finally, his hunger overtook him and he reached for the food in front of him. He kind of wished he still had his plate to fill.

"She's an observer. She studies all the plants in the garden. It's her job to know how to best use them," Noel said taking her last bite of rhubarb pie. "I think this is her pie recipe."

"She tells people what to do with them? Isn't that kind of what you do, Noel?" Boone took another bite of the silvery white corn.

"Not really." Noel lifted her plate and walked away playfully annoyed with Boone. He watched as the observer collected the wooden dishes and utensils from the other garden workers who had finished their meal. Now he had two people he had to talk to, the observer, and the fallen lady who was nowhere to be seen.

After dessert, the gardener motioned for Boone to stand. Boone slowly stood to his feet, afraid that he might be in some sort of trouble. But what he found was exactly the opposite. "Mishpachah," the voice of the gardener rang out, "let us welcome a new leader!" The workers cheered. Some sang and even danced. A lady, about the age of his mother, pulled Boone off of his seat and spun him around in circles singing and dancing. His friends sang joyfully and clapped to the rhythm of the celebration. Case climbed up on the bench and began waving his arms as if he were conducting one huge choir. The festivities continued well into the night. The sound of the cascading falls in the background set the rhythm for the celebration of Boone's awakening.

"All of this is for me," Boone realized. He stopped thinking about the mission he had devised and planned so thoroughly during the meal. He was captivated and drawn into the celebration, and he quickly found it easy to put aside his anxiety and enjoy the festivities of the night.

Chapter 16

Boone lay in bed the next morning with his eyes closed, wishing that when he woke up he would be surrounded by his dirty laundry and unfinished homework. Last night was the most fun he had experienced in a long time. People were cheering for him, shaking his hand, hugging him, loving him, and thanking him. For a moment, he convinced himself that he was starting to like it. Then, as he watched his friends dancing and acting silly with one another, he remembered how they were changing and forgetting their home. He wanted his friends back, the friends that liked to go hiking, take bike rides, and share an Ale-8 soda. Briefly, he thought he could smell the sweet gingery scent of his favorite soft drink, but it silently slipped away as the hint of mint filled his room. The invader jolted him awake with a reminder of the sole way out. He sat upright in bed and looked directly into two blue eyes. "Do you give everyone a wakeup call?" he asked sarcastically.

"No son, just the ones who need it. You've got work to do today," the gardener said. He reached out his hand for Boone to grab. "Let's walk."

The soft glow of candlelight from the gardener's lantern bounced across the doorways of the marble dome rooms. Even in the early morning darkness, the garden was peaceful and welcoming. Together, they walked to the middle of the rope bridge and stopped. "You still want to go home?"

"I do," Boone answered looking dizzily down to the garden below.

"You will, son. We aren't keepin' ya here. You're here because you need to be. All of us will be, some of us longer than others. Some of us were born here, and others were here from the beginning, but each of us has to make a choice. Lead them, son. Deny yourself, and then you and your friends will be able to go." He walked away leaving Boone alone to look over the generous land below him.

Still confused, Boone went down into the garden to walk, to be alone, and to think. The mist from the river was beginning to lift and cast a sparkling glow on everything around him. "Cool," he thought. "I guess it does kind of look like diamonds and emeralds around here." As he wandered, Boone stopped occasionally to smell a cacao pod in anticipation of the chocolate that would be created from it, or listen to the buzzing of the bees. The grass carpet squished up between his toes as he walked through the orchards. Boone was fascinated with everything he passed.

It was hard to see without the gardener's light in the early morning mist. Suddenly, Boone heard the continuous rustling of plants behind him. Someone or something was following him. Boone stopped abruptly. His heart beat faster in his chest. The sound of slowly approaching footsteps grew closer. He hoped it wasn't one of the wolves the gardener had referred to the day before. As he waited, he anticipated that some worker would be in the area ready to save him.

"Excuse me," a familiar voice spoke behind him.

Boone twisted so fast that he nearly fell over his own feet. "It's you, the observer!"

"I am so sorry I scared you. I came to officially introduce myself. Sometimes leaders and observers work close together. Well actually, we all work together. Although, there are times when you might need my help or I might need yours. Anyway," she rambled, "I'm Cora."

"You have a name!"

"Of course I have a name. Do you not?"

"Sure, um, it's Boone, Boone Tackett," he said awkwardly. "So do I call you Observer or Cora?"

"It doesn't matter. You are a leader, so it is okay if you call me Observer, but my friends call me Cora."

"You have friends?" It hadn't occurred to him that even in the garden people might have real relationships.

"You are funny. Do you not have friends? I am no different than you are, Boone Tackett. We are both created the same except you lived in the world and I live here."

"But this is part of our world too. We are still on Earth...aren't we?"

Cora was giggling so hard that she could barely speak, "Boone Tackett! The world is what is outside of the garden, where you are from."

"Oh," he said scratching his head. "I have so many questions. Do you think you could answer some of them for me?"

"Maybe."

"Maybe?"

"I will answer what I know. Anything else, you can ask a keeper."

"I know one of those," Boone said sarcastically. He had a million questions for his new acquaintance. He especially needed to know what the connection was between the flower sewn on her gown and his arrival into the garden, but first he figured he had better get to know her. "So, how long have you been trapped here?"

"Trapped? I don't understand," she said bewildered.

"You know, when did you get here?"

"I have always been here. I was born here," she answered smiling softly.

"Oh…" Boone was embarrassed that he hadn't considered that as an option. "Let me try another one. What's the flower on your dress mean?"

"That one I know. It for us to remember that He planted the first garden and it was good. So, what is in the garden is good for us to use as well. We have to be observant and use it wisely."

"I think I kind of knew that. But…when I fell here, there was a flower. I touched it, and here I am," he said hoping to get more answers.

"It has been a very long time since anyone has entered the garden the way you did," she laughed again. "But if He wants you here, it doesn't matter how you come in!"

"You are saying there is more than one way in?" Boone asked louder than he had meant to. If there were more than one way into the garden, there would have to be more than one way out.

"I am sorry. I do not know *your* answer, maybe a keeper…"

"Hey, what are you doing?" Noel asked making Boone jump. He was surprised to see her. "I saw you walking out here with the gardener, but then I saw him walking back without you. I wanted to make sure that you . . . . " She stopped when she saw Cora standing beside Boone, "Oh hello, Observer."

"Keeper, you have made perfect time! Boone Tackett has a question for you," Cora announced excitedly.

"Let me guess, Boone Tackett, you want to know how to get home," Noel predicted with her arms crossed across her chest.

Cora looked at Boone surprised, "Why do you want to leave if He brought you here?"

Boone was speechless. She was so disturbed at the thought of him or anyone, for that matter, wanting to leave the garden.

The mist was all around them now, creating the light that filled the entire cave. Noel spoke up, "So Boone, why do you want to leave?"

Now Cora was the one who was without words. "It was nice to meet you, Leader. I have to go." She turned and walked towards the center of the garden. Workers from all over settled into their day with the rising of the mist. They were all doing the job that each knew how to do and enjoyed doing the most. Singing voices were beginning to fill the air. The garden was alive.

"Cora, wait," Boone called to her, but she had already gone away. "Why did you make her leave?"

"What? I didn't make her leave. You and your questions made her leave. Don't ask her anything else. I'm your helper. I'm the one you need to ask," Noel stated matter of fact. "I have to get some sleep."

"Sleep? It's morning!"

"Like I told you before, someone is in the hall all the time; it was my turn last night. See you around…Boone Tackett," she chuckled.

"But what am I supposed to do? The gardener said to help my friends!" he called after her.

Noel turned back around with a big grin. "Boone, I will make it my personal mission to find out."

"Great," Boone said satisfied that something was going his way. He was glad that he didn't have her job. Sleep had always been number two on his priority list, closely following his number one, eating. Boone meandered throughout the garden without a clear compass. "Okay, help my friends, help my friends. The gardener said that's what I am supposed to do." He surveyed the area around the pumpkin patch where he had seen Wayne, and then to where he had seen Case. They were nowhere to be found. He strolled aimlessly farther and farther until he came to an area of the garden he had not yet seen, an enormous piece of unused land. It was not full of growing things or blossoming trees. It was soil, unused, empty, and to Boone, very boring. Amidst the dirt, Wayne and Case stood intensely in thought.

"Hey guys!" Boone yelled to them.

"Hey B!" Case replied. Boone proceeded towards them, moving watchfully in the gritty soil.

"What are you guys doing here?"

"Wayne's checking the soil to see if it has rested enough and I am here to keep him company," Case informed Boone.

"That doesn't look like work. Does the gardener know you are here?"

"Don't know." Wayne ran his fingers through the soil. "I knew it needed to be checked, so I came and did it. He didn't have to tell me to do something I knew needed to be done."

"The gardener told us that sometimes working means supporting someone else when they're doing their job. So, here I am," Case commented paying close attention to what Wayne was doing.

Boone was excited to have some time alone with the guys. "Great! Count me in! I came to help you. We can hang out like we used to."

"That's okay, Leader. You probably have other work to do. We'll meet up with you later." Wayne finally looked up from his work. "Case, I think it's time to plant. We'll send for some planters in the morning. It's rested enough."

"Aren't you allowed to take breaks?" Boone asked.

"You don't get it," Case stressed. "This is what we want to do. We're happy here. Nobody is making us work. We want to. It makes us feel good. We take a day of rest on our seventh, and we're good to go."

Case was right; Boone didn't get it. He had grown up with Sunday being church day, their official day of rest. It was something he was told to do, and not something he really wanted to do because most of the time it wasn't that restful. Waking up early, rushing off to church, coming home and doing homework, and then going to bed early because he had school the next day was in no way a day off for him. Boone didn't know what day it was in the garden. He had never heard anyone mention if it was a Tuesday or a Friday.

Turning his back on his friends, he walked away kicking up the loose soil as he went. Boone spent the rest of the day trying to find things to do. Unsure of how or even whom he was supposed to lead, he found himself roaming around with his hands in his pockets watching people. He hoped they would ask him for help but they didn't. They smiled, waved, and said things like, "Good morning, Leader" and, "We're glad to have you, Leader." The highlight of his day was when a lady offered for him to taste a strawberry that had she had just picked.

Boone continued this for most of the day, wanting someone to give him something to do. He tried to help his friends, but they didn't seem to want him around. Noel, he assumed, was either fast asleep or preoccupied with her books and couldn't possibly need him. Cora, however, had lived in the garden her whole life and said leaders and observers worked together. She had to know something he could do.

He searched the entire garden for her, asking workers of every type if they had seen her, but no one had. Eventually, he wandered over to the river that created a boundary between the garden and the forbidden pennyroyal. The smell made him sick, but he sat down anyway.

"It is not safe to be so close," Cora's soft voice startled him. "I heard you were wanting to see me. Why are you here?"

"I don't know where else to go, and it's quiet here," he said with his head between his knees. She sat down beside him and breathed in the air. "Doesn't the smell make you sick?"

"It could if I chose to breath in the penny flowers. Instead, I try to smell the strawberries and the honey. I love the smell of the honey. You are choosing what to breath," she explained looking out over the waters. For a few minutes they didn't speak. "Leader, why do you want to go home? You would not be here in our Mishpachah if at your center you did not want to be."

"My center?"

"Of course, we all have a center. It is your compass. Everyone who finds the garden has one. Some people only stay for a short time. If you thought you might leave tomorrow, why would you not want to be a part of this? Even after living here my whole life, I still make a choice each morning as to how I want to live my day. One day, I may have to go, but I cannot understand that yet. Boone Tackett, you have to make a choice, but that choice will not determine how long you will stay. The fruit of your choice determines that."

Boone soaked up every word Cora had for him. It was as if he had been offered a second chance at really seeing the garden. He was afraid to take it and embrace it. He was afraid that if he did he would never go home. "But what do I do? What do leaders do?"

"It is different for every leader, and depends on who you have chosen to lead. My father was a leader. Sometimes, he would lead the same way every day. Other times, each day was different."

Boone liked the excitement in her eyes when she talked about her father. It made him miss his own family. "You said your father *was* a leader?"

"His season changed when I was born. He is a puller now."

"Your dad went from a leader to a puller!"

"Boone Tackett, no one job is greater than another. We need them all. Without one, the others would not be successful. We work together."

The mist was going down and the smell of warm biscuits and grilled pineapples filled the mid-day air. "Thanks," Boone said standing to his feet. "I'll keep all that in mind." He had told Noel he would give the garden a chance, but he knew that he hadn't meant it. Now he understood that it might be the only way to get home.

Chapter 17

The next morning, Boone found that his first thoughts were not of home, but of Cora. Everyone in the garden had been calling him Leader. But when she said it, it was like she knew something about him that he didn't know, some secret that made him better than the person he thought he was. "Today," Boone said to his shadow, "I'm going to lead." He quickly jumped out of bed. The mist pouring through the opening in his ceiling glowed brighter, the air seemed clearer, and he was actually happier. He stepped out into the garden and greeted a puller with, "Good morning, keep up the good work."

The puller didn't seem at all surprised at the change in Boone. He tipped his straw hat, and said, "Good morning, Leader." On this day, the mint didn't bother Boone. The smell didn't make him nauseous or dizzy. He chose to smell something else, something sweet, like honey. The leader walked proud and happily through the garden enjoying the order that the garden produced. The smell of warm muffins and homemade jams from the morning's breakfast floated down from the preparation dome on the cliff.

Workers were busy pruning the grape vines and picking oranges. Some were planting seeds for the next season's harvest. Boone watched as a healer and a puller wandered arm in arm together happily talking. In fact, everyone he saw looked happy. He stopped to look around at the enormous cave ceiling that enclosed the garden and the towering falls that nourished it. Smiling with pride, he stepped forward. His foot made contact with a large mound on the ground causing him to trip and fall face first onto freshly tilled soil. Rattled and dirt covered, Boone got back on his feet. As he dusted the earth and mud off of his overalls, he returned to inspect the thing that had caused him to lose his balance. He leaned in close and then screamed, "Aaahhhh!"

"What? What's going on?" Case jumped up from his bed of lettuce leaves.

"Case? What are you doing on the ground?"

"Sleeping? What are you doing stepping on me?"

Boone eyeballed his friend curiously. "Why are you sleeping out here? Don't you have a room?"

"Of course I have a room, but I like it out here better. And besides, Wayne snores so loud that I haven't had a good night sleep in weeks, maybe days, or however long we've been here. Who knows?" Case said smiling and dusting off his own overalls.

"Everyone else is awake. Shouldn't you be singing or something?"

"Well, I was thinking about what you asked us yesterday. You know…about taking breaks. We get to officially rest a whole day each week, but we don't always get the same day as everyone else. I had my day, but Wayne worked that day and then he took the next day off. No one told us to do it. We knew we needed to rest, so we did. But, I got to thinking, what if we could all hang out like we used to. You know, hang out here, in this place that our parents have told us stories about since we were kids. We need to have fun…together! Do we really want to get back some day and say all we did was work? There are all these other people that are singing around here," Case said motioning to a nearby musician. "If I take another break here and there, it won't be a big deal. So, I was thinking that maybe we could hang out or something? What do you think?"

"Is this your, what did you call it? Your seventh?"

"Nope, it's my fourth."

"Your fourth?"

"You know, my fourth day of the week."

"Isn't today everyone's ones fourth day, like Thursday?"

Case squinted at Boone oddly. "You have got to catch up! Of course not! How long have you been awake? A day or two?"

"Something like that," Boone answered.

"So you're on your second."

Boone was starting to understand the timeline. "So if I'm on my second and you're on your fifth, then we'll never have time to hang out, right?"

"Exactly! There are celebrations, and the evenings, meals, days we finish early, and all the time we get to work together. Actually, we get to hang out a lot, but what if we want to hang out right now? Why should we wait? It's not like we're going to get detention," Case prodded.

"So, you think it's okay for us to do this?" Boone asked.

"You're a leader, you tell me."

Again, Boone was being asked to make a decision. He did want to hang out with the guys, and the gardener said to help them. Maybe this is what he wanted them to do. Maybe they had been working too hard. Maybe they had earned their fruit, or whatever Cora had told him, and now it was time to rest.

Boone looked up to see a tall figure walking his way. At first he thought it was the gardener, but immediately recognized his long time friend, Wayne. "Awesome morning! What are you doing here, Boone?"

"I kind of tripped over Case on my way to work," Boone answered. He was surprised at how easily the word work came out of his mouth.

"Great, I'm working on the new field today, helping a couple planters. See you around?"

"We're taking the morning off, Wayne!" Case shared excitedly. "Our leader and dear friend Boone said we could. Awesome, right?"

"That's not what I said, Case. You said you rested sometimes," Boone corrected. "I wanted to hang out with you, like we used to, that's all!"

"Are you sure we won't get in trouble, Boone? It's only my fifth and I feel fine. Is it okay with the gardener?" Wayne asked, looking around the garden to see who was listening.

Boone decided that this was the time to take charge. He woke up saying he was going to lead, so that's what he was going to do. After all, he was helping his friends. "No, we won't get in trouble. We'll hang out for a few minutes, thirty at the most, and then we'll get back to the garden. I'm a leader, right?" he said returning purposely to the ground and motioning for the others to sit too.

"Now he thinks he's important," Wayne teased. "He's the *leader*, so we all have to listen." Boone loved having the old Wayne back.

"What is so funny?" the voice of Cora interrupted them, "Why are you all lying down?"

"Hey Cora!" Boone was excited to see her and introduce her to his friends. "We're taking a break. You know, having fun. These are my friends, Case and Wayne. They came when I did."

"Hello, it is nice to know your names. Leader, it is morning. Most of us have not started our day yet. I do not understand."

"It's okay. Come hang out with us," Boone suggested. "You won't have to stay long."

"I am not sure . . . " she started to say.

"This is so much better than carrying water to the other workers. I say we do this every day!" Wayne interrupted.

"We have to do this at least once a day!" Case suggested.

"Count me in," Wayne confirmed. "You in, Boone?"

"I don't know," Boone said feeling oddly uneasy about it.

"We can start meeting after lunch. We'll take a break, and hang out. It will be fun," Case suggested. "Cora, what do you say?"

"Well, it is good to rest. Leader, what do you think?" her voice questioned.

"Yah, sure, I guess," he said fidgeting with a lettuce leaf. Something about this wasn't quite right.

"We should be somewhere more private, on the far side of the orchard by the falls edge," Cora suggested.

"Alright, we're set!" Wayne confirmed.

"Sure," Boone hesitantly approved. "I'll see you later." On the bright side of this, he would get to see his friends more and be with Cora. He had so much more he wanted to learn from her. However, his first official act as a leader didn't feel as satisfying as he had planned, and now he had no idea what else to do.

Boone weaved through the garden giving compliments, helping the workers with their odd jobs, and even spending some time walking and singing with Case. Boone felt taller now, smarter, and much more important. He wished the kids at school, or better yet, Ms. Shelly, could see him like this, leading and in charge. That would show her that he knew how to take pride in his work. At one point, Boone even passed the gardener with a smile, and said, "Hello, Gardener!"

"Well, hello, Leader. You are in good spirits this morning," the gardener said looking up from his seat in the grass. Beside him sat a lady. Her face was turned away from him and she didn't look up.

"I am, thank you." Boone peered down at the lady. Her appearance was very familiar to him, but seeing as how he didn't know many people in the garden, he couldn't quite place her.

"How is your work going today?" Boone questioned, sounding as official as possible. She wouldn't look up at him, but over to the gardener who answered for her.

"Our healer is doing much better," he assured. Boone turned his head sideways to get a better look at the lady. He did recognize her; it was the lady who had fallen.

"Hey, I know . . ."

The gardener stopped Boone from finishing his sentence. "Thank you. We are almost finished here," he said with his eyes focused on Boone's dark brown ones.

Boone got the hint and walked away. Occasionally, he peeked back and strained to hear what they were saying. Boone made a mental note to ask Cora about the healer. The day went on and Boone continued his leading. After lunch, he ran through the herb garden and across the bridge that led from the largest region of the garden, across the river, and to the orchard by the place where he and Cora had sat alone the day before. He had so many questions for her. When he arrived at the spot prearranged that morning, he found Case, Wayne, and Cora already lying in the grass and gazing at the cave roof. The roar of the falls was louder here than anywhere else. He could feel the sprays of the crashing water on his face.

"How long have you been here?" Boone asked annoyed that he wasn't notified of the time change.

"Calm down, Leader," Wayne said smartly. "We got here a little bit ago."

"Breath it in, Boone. Breath it in," Case instructed.

Boone lay down on the grass beside the group. As he inhaled deeply, the strong mint scent filled his nostrils and lungs. Boone sat up straight, coughing and nearly choking.

Cora sat up beside him and smacked him heavily on the back. "Are you okay, Leader? Think about something else; think about the lemongrass and the orange blossoms."

Case closed his eyes and hummed. His fingers drummed the green grass beneath him. "You did it too fast. Slow down."

Boone concentrated on the other smells of the garden as he had been instructed. It was like a whirlwind of scents floating in and out of the air. It soothed every inch of him as he lay in the bliss of rest and friendship. It was perfect. If Noel and Kaylee were here as well, all would be right.

The voice that he thought had abandoned him returned without forewarning. This time the voice was louder and stronger. "*You are him. You are him. You are him, Leader!*" He sat up again and looked at his friends. They hadn't heard it. He stood to his feet to see if maybe someone was hiding behind an orange tree. The others were now sitting up and looking up at him.

"Are you hearing things again?" Wayne asked.

"No, I don't think . . . " Boone answered, still looking around like he would see the source of the voice.

Cora got up and brushed grass clippings off her dress. "Leader, I think you have been too close to the penny field for too long. It takes wisdom and time before you are not taken by it. We are closer than most dare to get."

"Oh, no, I'm fine," Boone assured her. "Tired, but fine. I better get back to the garden." He couldn't believe that he just said that. *Get back to the garden?* He needed to get away from this spot. Boone waved and left quickly.

When he returned to the garden, he resumed his leading, walking, and waving. He occasionally stopped to help by giving an encouraging word, helping to carry a basket of fruit, or even humming a song. He was proud of how he had spent his day. Now, all he had to do was figure out how to deny his self and he could go home. However, that night, as Boone washed the dirt off of his feet with the warm washcloth and bowl of lavender water that had been left outside his door, he realized that he was becoming comfortable in this place where everyone loved him. No one thought he was changing, or expected him to know all the answers. *I think that maybe I could stay a few more days*, he told himself before climbing in bed and falling asleep.

It had been a week or more since they had begun their ritual of resting. Boone had actually lost track of what day he was on. It might have been his seventh, but he didn't know. Each day he woke up, went to the garden, and greeted the workers. He complimented the way workers trimmed the lemongrass, helped pick a few apples, and carried baskets of corn or cucumbers to the kitchen. Then he would run to meet the others in the orchard by the falls. Everyday was becoming the same, he was falling back into a comfortable routine, and he liked it.

Since he no longer knew what day it was, he believed it was time to take a seventh. At home he would have slept in, gone to church, and come back home. This day, he planned to spend his seventh by surprising his friends and being the first to arrive. But when he reached the falls they were already there lying in the grass, staring at the cave ceiling, and laughing. He knew that they had been coming to the falls earlier and staying longer. Even he had found himself there when the mist started settling to the ground.

Wayne was making a conscious effort to make Cora laugh, and Case would break out in song pulling for a compliment from her. Boone sat down and leaned back against a pomegranate tree to watch the water crash to the ground. He didn't have anything that would impress Cora, no jokes or musical talent. He still wanted to ask her about the fallen woman, but it never felt like the right time.

"*You are him, Leader*," the voice inside him returned. He tried to ignore it by laughing out loud at Wayne's jokes, but the voice had embedded itself within him with no intention of letting go. He tried to distract his mind by thinking of ways to grab Cora's attention. He had to do something that would set him a part from the others. Silencing the voice inside, he had an idea.

Boone woke wondering if he had actually slept at all. "Can somebody turn off the light?" he moaned shielding his eyes. "Let me sleep just a little longer." He shivered, and reached down to pull his sheet up over his body, but it wasn't there. With his eyes closed to block out the light he felt around for his missing blanket. His bed felt funny, not really like a bed at all. The more he thought about it, it didn't smell like his room either. He had become accustomed to waking to the scents of fresh pastries and warm muffins, but what he smelled didn't smell very good at all. It was strong and overbearing. Boone wrinkled his nose and sat up, realizing that he had spent the night outside by the falls.

He rubbed his aching head and looked around at Case, Wayne, and Cora who were fast asleep by the waters edge. He didn't remember falling asleep last night. For that matter, he didn't remember much of anything about the evening before. "Case," Boone called giving his musical friend a gentle nudge. "Wake up!"

"The sun shines bright," Case sang in his sleep.

Boone tried again. "Case, we're outside! Wake up!"

"Mom, I don't want to go to zoo," Case whined still sleeping. Boone gave up on his sleeping friends. He would find out later what had happened the night before, and why they had not made it back to their domes.

He stood up and stretched. His body ached and his stomach growled with intense hunger. He couldn't remember what he had eaten for dinner. Boone yawned and proceeded to walk to breakfast. He felt grimy and could taste that he needed to brush his teeth. The light in the garden seemed brighter than usual; he wished he had a pair of sunglasses.

The last thing he remembered was taking a seventh to be with his friends. As he walked, workers lifted their heads and eyed him strangely. He rubbed his thick curly hair curiously, and continued towards breakfast. The mist was high and in full glow. Its brightness was beginning to annoy him.

He was just about to climb the spiral staircase when a little voice called to him. "Excuse me, Leader," a small boy said while tugging on his pants leg. "Will you show me the way to the berries?" Boone looked back on the garden. The berry patches were in the opposite direction he was going.

He heard his stomach moan. "They're that way," he said pointing off into the distance.

"Will you take me?" the boy pleaded.

Boone bit his lip. *Surely the kid can find it on his own,* he thought. *There are plenty of workers in the garden who could help him.* "It's not that far," Boone said. "I have to go, maybe next time." He ran up the stairs without looking back on the boy. He knew he should have taken him, but it could have taken at least thirty minutes to get there and back. He was afraid he might miss out on breakfast, like he felt like he had on dinner. He couldn't wait to get his hands a maple syrup sticky bun.

The garden seemed busier than ever. He passed one of the other keeper's steading a tower of books, and a puller with his arms overflowing with baskets of newly harvested apples. *They're up early,* Boone thought strolling by.

He yawned again accidentally bumping into a musician who was being escorted by a healer. "Sorry," Boone mumbled sleepily.

The musician was rubbing his neck as the healer gave him orders. "Lemon and honey, four times daily, until you can speak again." The musician started to say something. "And none of that. No talking for at least three days." The musician nodded. "Don't know what's going on around here," the healer said. "I've been treating more people in the past week than I have in years."

When Boone arrived at the tables, only a few servers remained. "Where is everyone?" he asked frantically. "Where's breakfast?"

"Sorry, Leader," one of the servers said while setting the table with plates and bowls. "We're setting up for lunch."

Lunch? Boone thought. Had he slept through the morning? He was so hungry that he was becoming dizzy. How could twelve hours of his life be missing? He had to get back to Cora. He had to wake them up. He had to let them know. Something was very wrong.

Still hungry, Boone ran across the suspended bridge to the staircase. He stopped short at the top when the little boy from earlier stepped in front of him. "Please, Leader! Will you take me to the berries?"

Boone had started to really enjoy helping out in the garden. And on any other occasion, he would have gladly helped the little timer. "I can't do it right now!"

"But, Leader, they need me, I have to help."

"You're just a kid! They don't *need* you," Boone grumbled.

The boy looked hurt. "Yes they do. My mother said they needed more workers. I can work too." Boone sighed. He tried to decide what was more important, remembering where his night had gone, or taking this child in front of him to the berry patches. In his eyes he saw his sister Kaylee. He realized that he hadn't seen her in a few days.

"Fine," Boone groaned. He walked down the stairs with the mini-person at his heels. He didn't speak as they passed through the herbs and the vegetable rows. Boone was becoming irritated at all of the workers who were giving him funny looks. It was like he had an arm growing out of his head or something. He brushed down his hair and smoothed out his clothes. He even dusted off his backside, afraid that he might have sat on an overripe pomegranate during his missing hours.

When they arrived at the edge of the blackberry patch, Boone said, "Here you go."

The timer shuffled his feet in the dirt. "I don't know how to pick them."

"What?" Boone almost shouted drawing more eyes to his attention. "You had me drag you all the way down here, and you don't even know how to pick them?"

Tiny water droplets formed in the boy's eyes. "You are the leader. My mother said you could help me."

The voice that accompanied him returned, *You are him.* He almost pushed it away, when the idea of blocking it reminded him of his idea. He had to get back to them. He had to get them back to garden life. "I have to find someone, then I'll come back and show you how to pick. Is that okay?"

The boy wiped his forearm across his dripping nose. "As long as it's not past my bedtime."

Boone threw his arms up in the air. He was losing patience. "It won't be past your bedtime, okay!"

Just then, another timer walked his way. She held in one arm a baby, and in the other a basket of blackberries. "Is everything all right, little one?" she asked the boy as he ran to her side and buried himself under her apron. "Leader, is he burdening you?"

Boone's heart sank. "No, ma'am."

"We could use your help," she said calmly.

"I can't," Boone responded flatly. "It's hard to explain. I have to go." He took off toward the orchard to find the others.

He crossed the bridge into the orchard like he had done everyday since he had tripped over Case. As he passed the rows of brightly hued oranges and into the pomegranate trees, he could hear their laughter. They were still there. Boone picked up his pace. They had been there too long. This wasn't what he had intended when he had suggested they skip the day and stay until the mist fell.

This time when he arrived, the three were not lying on their backs looking up at the rock sky, but instead they were facing the falls. Cora was dreamily swirling her finger in the water. Boone knew that this was bad. His feet were frozen, planted in the ground, as he observed them laughing and breathing in the aroma of the forbidden field. "*You are him, Leader. Lead her,*" the voice inside urged. He knew he should say something to her. Cora splashed water at the boys playfully as she chattered on about growing up in the garden and never getting to see the world. Then he saw her stand. *Lead her. You are him!* he told himself. She placed a foot in the water and then stepped forward.

"No!" Boone yelled. He raced to her side, reached for her, and pulled her away from the water's edge.

"What is wrong with you?" Case said jumping to his feet and placing himself directly in front of Boone. "You totally freaked me out!"

"No kidding. Are you all right, *Leader?*" Wayne snickered.

"Leader," Cora whimpered, "I, um, I have to go. Sorry...I will see you tomorrow." Boone watched her run back through the trees.

"Cora wait!" he called. "I need to talk to you." But she was gone.

"This stuff really gets inside of you," Case said patting Boone on the back. "I don't think you should come back and hang with us. You made her leave."

"He's right. See ya around, Boone," Wayne said following after Case.

Slowly breathing in, Boone allowed the mint filled air to invade him. It made him feel angry again. *What had happened to them last night?* he wondered. On his walk back to the garden, he replayed the incident with Cora. "I think I'm crazy," he laughed at himself. "She was just putting her foot in the water. It's not like she was going to the field."

At dinner that night, Wayne and Case didn't speak to him. Occasionally, one of them would glance up at him and then return to whisper to the other as if in a secret conspiracy against him. They ate quickly and left. Noel and Kaylee were nowhere to be seen. Actually, he hadn't seen Kaylee at dinner for at least a week. Assuming that she wasn't hungry or that he might have missed her, he continued to eat his rosemary potatoes and roasted corn on the cob. He was so hungry that he couldn't seem to quench his hunger.

Noel appeared beside him. "B, enough is enough! Look at you. You're sluggish and worn down. You look like you haven't slept in days! What have you been doing, or should I say what haven't you been doing?"

Boone recalled that Wayne and Case had looked tired. In fact, everyone at the table appeared weary and beat up. Their eyes were darkened with lack of sleep and they ate slower and quieter without the usual laughter and excitement of sharing the accomplishments of their day. He wondered if he looked the same. "Hey N, glad someone is talking to me."

"Boone, I actually do need to talk to you. It's really important." He kind of feared that she had found a way home.

"Not now."

"Boone, here," Noel dropped a book in his lap. "You need this."

"I don't need help. I've got this leader thing down."

"Obviously, you do need my help. Look at everyone!" He looked up again at their exhausted faces. Even she looked tired. "What does this have to do with you?"

"It's *my* job, Boone. Remember me, your *best* friend?" She pointed down at the book. The book was all too familiar to him. It was one of the red leather books, and it bore the tree of life marking, the same tree that marked him as leader among the others. In the past week, he had slowly forgotten about their quest for the mythical world, their church, their families, and his home. He smiled up at Noel, remembering how it all began, but she didn't smile back. "I really don't need your help," he yelled to her jokingly.

"You do!" she yelled back.

He opened the book, turned the page and read: "To the leader of the called out ones." He took his final bite of fried apples and ran back to his room, eager to read more about his position. "Be on guard," he read, "for yourselves and for all the flock, among which the Holy Spirit has made you overseers, to shepherd the church of God which He purchased with his own blood. I know that after my departure savage wolves will come in among you, not sparing the flock." This couldn't be right. Why should he be on guard? He had to keep reading. "To the leader as is written in the Acts be on guard for a member of the body can weaken the entire body, as the body is one." The words *weaken* and *wolves* coursed through him bringing back images of his nightmares.

As the impact of the words began to sink in, Boone realized what had happened. He had allowed not one member of the garden to fall, but three. While Boone and his friends took the day off, the other members were working harder and harder to make up for the work that was not being done. If one member weakened the body, what would three do? In the faint distance, he heard a sound that made him afraid. A far off howl echoed through his room, followed by screams of dread.

Chapter 18

Boone felt sick, really sick. His body was sweating, the pain in his temples pulsated, and his insides were coiled into knots. What had he done? What had he not done? His lack of real leadership had brought terror to the whole garden. He knew he should have stepped up. He knew he should have taken charge. Why did he let them lay around all day? For that matter, why had he suggested they stay into the night?

Not doing their job had weakened everyone. It was so clear to him now. The workers did what they were supposed to do; they weren't expected to do the work of those who decided they didn't want to. The gardener had warned him, but Boone hadn't listened. He led, but did so in a way that would make *him* happy. He led the way he wanted to, not in a way that was best for the garden. His friends were happier before he had tried to change them.

The howls outside his room grew louder. Boone hadn't seen a single animal since he had been there. He couldn't image what he had brought upon the garden! He feared the worst as the moans and yelps of untamed beasts bounced off of the cave walls.

As his eyes filled with tears, Boone saw the gardener running towards him. "I'm sorry," Boone cried.

"No need, son. They are coming to lift you," he spoke directly to Boone in a tone that neither implied anger or frustration.

"Let me help. Let me lead. I know what to do now. I can help!" Boone begged.

The gardener placed his hand on Boone's shoulder. "No Leader, you have fallen. There are those who can help, but not you. You cannot help with this. You need to heal, Boone. Do you hear? They are close and they will destroy us if they aren't stopped," the gardener said sternly. The screams of workers intertwined with the shrill of the invaders. "Leader, they are already here." He turned briskly and excused himself through the entrance to Boone's room.

"Fallen?" Boone asked. It hadn't dawned on him that by letting the others fall, he had fallen as well. Boone barely had time to stand to his feet when several workers rushed through his door. Everything started to happen so fast that he couldn't count how many there were. The hands of the workers lifted him above their heads; among the hands were Noel's. "You have to put me down! I caused this. I can fix it. Let me do my job!"

"No Boone," she said harshly.

"N! Please, you have to let me help. I can fight. I can fix this."

"Boone, stop! This is how it is done. This is how it works."

"Fine!" He yelled. "Put me down!" He flailed his arms and legs attempting to break loose of the hands that protectively restrained him. The breeze of the night air flowed above and below him. Then, he heard his sister scream. "That's my sister! Kaylee! It's okay! I can fix this!" He felt helpless. The power he had enjoyed a day before was gone. He turned his head as the lifters carried him through the garden. Workers all over the garden were engaged in combat with something large. He tried to get a better look, but they were moving too fast. Howls continued to surround him. The screams terrified him.

Boone struggled to sit up. Then, he saw it, a beast, half wolf, half human. Its hair hung long, gray streaked with a red the color of fire. Its body towered above the worker on two hind legs. Long black nails grew from hands that were large and manlike. The wolf roared revealing a mouth full of fangs and jagged teeth. It was exactly as he had dreamed. Boone tried to kick again to free himself. He wasn't afraid of what would happen to him, but he feared what would become of this place that thrived on praise, growth, and service to others.

Ahead of him was the large dome shaped room where Noel had kept the books. He was heading there. As the howling increased so did the number of creatures that Boone could make out. They ripped and tore at the garden, uprooting berries, and destroying herbs. It hurt him to see all that hard work reduced to broken twigs. The lifters picked up their pace as the wolves closed in on them. They used free arms to push and shove the large creatures away, and took whatever scratches and injuries were inflicted upon them without stopping for even a second.

As the breeze increased, Boone could make out the scent of mint filtering from the pennyroyal. It was stronger and more intoxicating than it had ever been. The doorway was close; he could see it up ahead. The wolves were on them now, but he was still moving. A pair of hands that had been holding tightly to his legs was suddenly yanked away leaving his leg drooping and exposed. The howls and the screams were deafening. More hands left him as the wolves pulled at the lifters.

"They want you!" Noel screamed. "They won't hurt you! But what they will do is much worse! Hang on!"

"Go! Run!" a lifter at his right shoulder yelled to the other three that remained. They were still holding Boone in their arms as they pushed themselves to move faster. From the corner of his eye, Boone could see a dark haired wolf running towards him on all fours. The dome was footsteps away, but the wolf was gaining on them. He looked back again and saw two menacing green eyes declaring him as their host's target. Their fascinating glare beamed in the glow of the mist as it ran alongside him. There was something oddly beautiful to Boone about the threatening creature.

Noel tried to fight the wolf away with her free arm, but the eyes of the wolf would not detach their hold on him. Their green glow was hypnotic; he didn't want to stop looking. The deeper he fell into the eyes, the easier it was for him to see his own reflection. The wolf entranced Boone with its familiarity until it violently smacked at his face creating a line of blood down his cheek. He could see bodies being thrown up into the air all around him with faint life visible in each one. Noel held tighter to him.

They were at the doorstep to the dome. The shadowy wolf reached for Noel's arm, forcing her to lose her hold. As she dropped Boone heavily at the doors entrance, the wolf jumped over her and lunged at him. A set of arms wrapped around the wolf and pulled it to the ground. In all the disorder he thought his mind might be playing tricks on him, as the person he saw connected to those arms was Jeff.

"No!" Boone screamed. He stumbled to Noel, grabbed her by the arm, and pulled her into the room with him. "We can't be safe in here!" Boone pleaded with Noel. "We have to leave, now!" He put his head in his hands to focus on what had just happened. "Was that Jeff?"

"No, I mean…yes. This is where you have to be. They won't touch the books," Noel replied. "They're afraid of them, afraid of what they might say."

"What? Who are they? People are hurting, maybe dying for all we know. I can't be here! I need to be out there!"

Noel stopped in front of the doorway. "No, you have to be here."

"How do you know all this?" Boone asked trying to catch his breath.

"It's my job, Boone."

"Your job! Wayne is probably dead out there, eaten by some wolf man monster. As for Jeff, I don't even know how he got here, and all you can say is it's your job! Why won't you let me help?" He was now furious.

Noel lowered her head as tears flowed down her face. She slid to the ground and leaned against the marble wall. "You fell, Boone. You stayed there too long. You didn't do your job, you put us all in danger . . . and you put yourself in danger, Boone."

"This is out of control!"

"Look at your hands, Boone," Noel wept. He lifted his hands in front of his face. His fingernails had started to grow yellow and dark. He flashed back again to the dream he had of himself face-to-face with the beast. "Don't you see? When they stopped working, the fruits that they were nourishing started to die; it's the fruit that keeps all of us going. With no fruit, we are not sustained. The garden became weak and vulnerable. When you fall, you have to be lifted, cared for, and taught again until you are ready to serve again. If not, you go deeper into their world. Boone, the wolves consume people with their ideas and their ways, until we become them. They are what is inside of us until we choose to accept a new life. When we forget what we have chosen, this new life, we begin to feed on the chaos. We grow wild and ravaging. We change and take what is not to be taken."

"So, I'm becoming one of them!"

"You were, Boone, until we lifted you. You didn't even see the changes in you. Kaylee saw them first and it scared her."

"So that's why she stopped coming to dinner," he said under his breath. "What about Wayne and Case?"

"We didn't get to them in time," she sobbed. "Case fought the lifters away, and Wayne...he ran, he ran from them. I think they were planning to come for you. I didn't see him until a few minutes ago." The screams and howls remained, filling the mist of the evening.

"Are you saying those monsters are our friends? And that thing that tried to take my arm off was…"

"Boone, I'm so sorry. I know you liked her," Noel comforted with reddened eyes. "We all did."

"That was Cora? But she lives here. She was born here. How could it happen to her?"

"She was taken by something else, something much stronger, Boone. She let the pennyroyal get to her. She came to me asking how to make the voices stop. She said they called her to it. I read everything I could. I've been studying the plant ever since we got here. I've looked at samples and read the books. I tried to talk to her, to calm her down, but she wouldn't listen. She kept crying and saying she knew she shouldn't go back. She knew what was happening. She didn't want to, no one does, but she fell to it…to some it's faster than others. Boone, you didn't do your job. So she didn't do hers. Look," she shoved a red book in his face.

"For the body is not one member but many," he read. It was difficult to concentrate through the sounds of the continuing chaos outside. "And if one member suffers all the members suffer with it." He shut the book. His face flushed with anger, mostly at himself.

"It's from the ancient scrolls, Boone," she added quietly.

"I know . . ." he did know. He had heard it before, but that Wednesday night in youth group, the night he and Jeff had gotten in a fight, he could have cared less what it said. Now, it was like a light had turned on in front of him.

"They all are, Boone. These books that I read have nothing really to do with pulling weeds and pruning herbs. Every single one of them has to do with life. It's about how the workers live, how they work, and how they function alone and with each other. The workers come seeking answers and this is where I tell them to find them. Sometimes I show them, but they have to read it and understand it for themselves. You may have led them, but they are responsible for their decision to follow. Take responsibility for what you have done."

Tears had not stopped pouring from Noel's eyes. He didn't mind them now or seeing this side of her. He knew the tears were more out of fear for his life than what was going on outside. "I've destroyed the garden. There's nothing I can do. If I can't do anything to fix this, then why did they want me?"

"They want you because you are the one who can put it all back. You are their leader. The selfishness inside of them wants to drag you with them. You are not ordinary, Boone Tackett. You have changed. Don't you feel it?"

Boone did feel different, but it was a difference he was not ready to accept. He stared oddly at the walls filled with red books. "I still have so many questions!"

"Not all questions are meant to be answered the moment you have them. Sometimes a person isn't ready to hear the answer they need."

He took her by her hands and lifted her to her feet. "Thanks for not giving up on me. I truly am sorry for all of this." As if his words had pushed a mystic mute button, the uproar outside vanished into an unnatural silence. Boone held his breath, afraid that breathing the wrong way might bring back the destruction. Noel sat down behind a wooden desk piled high with books. A nearly melted beeswax candle dimly lighted the area. As if nothing had ever happened, she began to pour through the scriptures before her, like Boone had seen her do on many Sunday mornings.

"What happened?" Boone asked peaking outside the door. "Everything stopped." He placed his ear near the door's opening. "Is that humming? Are they singing?"

Noel smiled. "Yes."

"But, where did they go?"

"They're still here."

"What?"

"Leader," the gardener's presence and exhausted voice was unexpected. "It is safe for you now." His work clothes were torn and blood stained. Boone stepped outside to see near lifeless bodies being carried to various domes. The wolves were nowhere in sight, except for one. It was Cora. Before Boone could even ask, the gardener spoke, "She will be cared for as we cared for the women you saw the day you awoke. It will take some time before we let her work, but she is our family, our Mishpachah, and we love her as we love you. It may take her longer than the others, but she'll heal as long as we don't forget that healing is what she needs."

"She could have killed you. Look! You're bleeding!"

"No," the gardener comforted, "they cannot take this life that you see. She caused a lot of pain, but the pain that we feel from losing her for a while is much, much greater. Let's walk, Leader." The gardener walked ahead of Boone and then turned back to look at Noel. "Thank you for restoring our leader. He still needs some work, but a job well done."

Boone smiled back at his helper and followed the gardener as he led the way. All around them, workers were busy in the garden replanting uprooted vines, pruning broken limbs, and harvesting fruit that had fallen to the ground. The gardener led him to the spot where day after day he had watched his friends turn into wolves, and he had been blind to it all.

"Leader, it is sometimes hard to tell when someone is being led astray. Often the tasks we are called to do for the family change, and we change with them. It can make others think we are not doing what we should, but that person alone knows what he's truly called to do. If we're doing that task and doing it well, then we're succeeding for those within the family, and those on the outside as well. Beyond the pennyroyal is a field far worse, far more tempting, but desperate and thirsty for the life we know. That is where you are from, and that is where the man Elijah Craig is from."

Boone was shocked to hear his name. He had forgotten all about him and his fairy tale. "He was really here?"

"A long time ago, Leader. He was a leader like you, called to us to learn how to lead. He stayed for a long time. But then, he was called out when he learned to deny himself. It is what you will have to do. The way out is different for all of us. Some of us come and go often; others work here to help those outside. Do you understand, Leader?"

"I don't know…I think so. If this place is supposed to help people, then why keep it hidden from everyone?"

"We are not hidden Leader, the world is blind. Some may try to hide us, but people like you, will always hear us. Elijah was a man of great heart, but he was also a man of business. He had plans for the Mishpachah that were his way and not ours. Some of his family remained here and others went back to protect it and share the beliefs of the Mishpachah. Although many have passed on, they have left you with what I believe you call your Great Crossing, a church."

The falls crashed down ahead of him, repeatedly pouring water from the cave opening. Boone couldn't believe what he was hearing. "Jeff and his family are from the ones who went back with Craig, aren't they?" The pieces of the mystery were coming together - the necklace, the picture, and the hidden library. It all made sense.

"That's correct. He is the one who saw in you what you did not see in yourself."

"He recruited me?"

The gardener laughed, "If that is what you'd like to call it."

"But how did he get down here?"

"You will have to ask him yourself. Noel and your quest made it a lot easier for him to get you here."

"Easier! I almost died!"

"The garden wouldn't have let that happen." The gardener put his hands on Boone's shoulder. "I think that is enough for now. You still have to find your way back and lead your friends out, Leader." The softly glowing mist illuminated the workers repairing the damage that had been done to the garden. "Goodnight, Leader." The gardener left Boone alone with a lot to think about, including whether or not he even wanted to go back home.

Chapter 19

Boone entered the healing room uncertain of what to expect. The gardener's lesson hung like a cloud ready to burst inside his brain. It was still all a mess to him. He thought he was supposed to lead his friends *to* the garden. Then, he was told to lead them *in* the garden. Now, he was supposed to lead them *out?* This place was comfortable and peaceful. He didn't want to leave and face the stresses that ordinary life had placed upon him. He didn't want to have to deal with finishing English assignments or cleaning his room. Here he was a leader; he was celebrated and appreciated. So he messed up, but now he knew what to do and he wouldn't let it happen again. One day, he might even become like the gardener.

The healing room was warmer than he had expected. Wooden hospital beds poked out from the walls of the circular room. Fresh flowers filled the vases beside each of the occupied beds. Every bed was full of victims as a result of his fall. Not one was empty. Guilt started to overwhelm Boone. A group of people was laughing at the far back of the room. Boone trudged toward them, doubting that his presence would be received well. "Good morning, Leader," a voice halted him. Boone recognized him as one of his lifters. "I am glad you are well."

Boone stopped and eyed the wounded. "I'm sorry. What did you say?"

"I am glad you are better. You look good," the badly bruised leader painfully forced a smile.

"I feel better. How are you? I mean, are you hurting?"

"Nah, a couple broken bones, a bruise here, and a scrape there. Healer says I will be good as new in no time. She is something; knows how to use the plants of the garden better than anyone else. She must have spent hours with a keeper. When I first came here, I was real sick. I couldn't think straight, but she fixed me right up."

Boone hadn't met anyone else who had talked about coming here, other than Elijah Craig. But now, here was someone he could actually talk to. "So, you haven't always been here? How did you find it?"

The young man sat up slowly in his bed. His arm hung in a sling and a bandage wound neatly around his head. "I don't remember a whole lot. Like I said, I was really sick. My mom and dad worked with another family…"

"Wait, when you say *family*, do you mean there are more of these underground gardens?"

The injured started to laugh and then held his chest as if the laughter caused him more pain. "Leader, don't you know? There must be millions of families everywhere! We served far from here. Mom and dad were called here and so we came. Things changed a bit. Mom was a leader and dad a gardener. Now, they are back out there."

"You mean on the surface?"

"That's right; you're catching on a bit."

"But how did you get here?"

"Well, I think you know that," he laughed.

Boone frowned and lowered his head. "Yeah, I'm really sorry. But what I meant was…"

171

He laughed again, "I'm joking, Leader. I know what you meant. Truthfully, we walked right in. The door opened and we came in."

"Are you kidding me? There's a door?"

"Well, there was for us. I don't think it is the same for everyone. Probably not the answer you were looking for. Sorry, are you still trying to get out of here?"

"How did you know?" Boone asked.

The leader shrugged, "That's why most people fall. They either want to leave because they think things are better somewhere else and then they forget what they were supposed to be doing in the first place, or they want to do things their own way. It happens every once in a while."

"I don't know what I want." Boone stopped, not knowing why he was sharing this with someone he had only encountered once. "I really like it here. It makes sense. And I think I know what I'm supposed to do now. I want to stay, I think, but the gardener says I'm supposed to go."

"Well," he said becoming very serious, "I can't help you there. I will tell you this. We are all called to go at some point or other. No one should stay forever."

The familiar voice of the healer interrupted him, "That's enough, Leader."

"Oh, sorry," Boone said quietly stepping away.

"Ya need to rest, Leader." The healer easily plumped the injured's pillow and lifted a glass of water to his mouth. Boone realized that the leader she was talking to was not he at all, but the one who had tried to save him. Embarrassed, he turned and walked away.

"Hey, Leader," the bed ridden voice went on, "nice talking to you." Boone gave a nod to his new acquaintance and continued his journey to the end of the room.

"Boone!" the squeal of his sister echoed within the dome walls. He ran and jumped into his arms and held him tightly. He knew he was healing, because Kaylee no longer feared the sight of him. He held on to her and kissed her forehead. "I am so glad you are okay. You don't even look scary anymore! It's time to go home now, isn't it? Are you leading us home, Boone? The gardener said you would lead us home!"

Boone kept holding on. He didn't want to let go of her. "You like it here, don't you? Why do you want to go home?"

"I miss mommy and daddy," she whimpered, letting her bottom lip to protrude. "But the gardener told me we could come back anytime, so it's okay if we go. We can go now, can't we Bubby?"

"I don't know," he said honestly.

"Oh," Kaylee whispered. The laughter at the end of the room had started up again. He took the small hand so she could take him to where he could see Noel sitting on the side of a hospital bed. In the bed, Wayne lay with his face badly bruised. His eyes were barely visible through their swollen eyelids. Even from where he was standing, Boone could see that Wayne's fingernails still bore traces of being yellowed and black. He wasn't completely healed, but Boone knew from the laughter that Wayne's personality was returning to normal. As Boone came upon the group, he could see that the others around him were Case and Jeff. The sight of Jeff brought up old feelings of anger inside Boone, but more so his desire to interrogate him.

"Boone!" Case nearly shouted, jumping up from his bedside seat to hug him, and showing no trace of his very recent transformation. Case's greeting was followed by a hug from Noel, a nod from Jeff, and a pain filled grin from Wayne.

"What took you so long, Leader?" Wayne mumbled. "Couldn't decide what you were going to wear to come see me?" Everyone started laughing again. Boone looked down at his overalls, the same ones every other guy in the room wore, and grinned.

"It's good to see you, Wayne. Um, can I talk to you and Case alone for a minute?" Boone asked.

"Nope," Wayne answered sharply, but with a smile.

"No? But, I really need to talk to you and it's kind of between us."

"B, everyone here knows what you're going to say. Something like, 'I am so sorry this happened, you're my friends, we been friends since we was kids, so on and so forth'. Am I right? We're a family, Boone. There are no secrets. If there is anyone you need to talk to alone, I bet it needs to be our pal Jeff here," Wayne prompted still grinning with delight at the uncomfortable feeling he was giving Boone and the red glow of embarrassment that was forming on Jeff's cheeks.

"Yah, I guess that's it, except I would actually mean it."

"I know you would," Wayne said adjusting himself in the bed to find a more comfortable spot, "but it doesn't matter. We made our own decisions. I'm in this bed because I made a bad choice. You figured it out, Leader, and you didn't even know it. I felt it too, but I didn't say anything. Guess I should be the sorry one." That was the most serious Boone had ever heard Wayne be in his entire life. The room was now quiet. The light from the opening above was beginning to dim and the mist was setting.

"How come every time I have to come get my patients to rest, you are right there with them, Leader, keeping them awake." This time, the healer behind Boone was talking to him. "All right, all of you shoo. He's almost healed. It's that your lovin' on 'em, that helps them the most," she said picking up Wayne's hand and examining his nails. "Open up," she commanded Wayne. She investigated the places in his mouth where fangs had been the night before. "You awfully strong to be comin' together so fast. I'm proud of you, Timer." Boone still couldn't help but feel guilty. He smiled at Wayne. Wayne tried to smile back with his mouth still wide open and a healer looking into it.

Boone turned and followed Jeff, Noel, Case and Kaylee from the healing room as they smiled and chatted as if life was returning to the way it had always been. On his way out, Boone saw her. Just a few days ago she had been with the gardener. Her body showed no sign of being among those injured, but here she was, sleeping. "Excuse me," he asked a male healer. "How is she?"

"Our healer has her good days and her not as good days," the attendant said leaning over to check her pulse.

"So, she wasn't out there..." Boone didn't want to finish what he had to say. Thankfully, the healer finished his thought for him.

"No, Leader, she was here with us. Such a shame, she knows her ability well. She would have been a good help to us. I think people were healed just from the words she spoke over them. It was hard for me to believe sometimes, but it happened." The fallen women lay peacefully in her bed. "She won't speak to anyone, but the gardener now. Such a shame."

How ironic, he thought, *that a healer is here to be healed.* Boone had sought her out for answers, but from the looks of it, she didn't even have her own.

Boone exited into the cool still air of night. Across the garden, evidence of the battle he had created was still visible, but he could tell that like Wayne, it too was healing fast. Jeff was waiting outside for him and spoke first. "It's all right if you feel like you want to hit me. I think you probably played it over in your mind for a long time." Boone admitted to himself that he probably had imagined it a time or two. Once he saw that his life-long enemy was not about to knock him to the ground, Jeff continued. "I knew you would be called all along. I just didn't want to believe it."

"Jeff, you don't make any sense! The gardener said that you were the one who drafted me. So why try to get me in trouble with Reed, or scare me half to death in the church? Why not come out and tell me?"

Jeff snapped at him. "Would you have believed me, Boone? Ever since we were kids, I have tried to be your friend. I tried to be a part of your clique. I tried anything I could to get close to you so that you might at least listen. The only one of you that would even give me the time of day was Noel and you guarded her like she was a piece of gold! I knew that this was what you needed to see who you really are. I was the one who brought you before the gardener and he agreed. We had to get the timing right. That night in the church I wanted to tell you everything because I knew why you were there. I saw your drawings. It was then that I realized that you knew you were being called to serve in the garden. You were trying to find something that was greater than you!"

"So, why didn't you? Why let me fall through a hole in the ground, dragging everyone else with me. What would make you do that when I could come in the way you did?"

"That was kind of an accident that we hadn't planned on. The garden has its own way of getting people here, you were directed the way you were supposed to go. It's not like I can walk you through some magical front door. Well actually, there is a door, but you wouldn't have seen it because you didn't know what you were looking for. We could have been standing in front of it with me turning the handle and you still would have been blind. I don't know what you sensed, what you saw, or what you were told, but you got here because you searched for it. As for everyone else, you led them here because you are a leader, Boone. They followed you. They wouldn't have come on their own. Elijah Craig wanted to lead people here too, he really did, but his heart changed. Even if people had followed him, they couldn't have seen it for what it is! Don't you get it?"

"So the dreams, the visions, the nightmares...are you saying that was all inside of me and I saw all of that because I wanted to?"

"Boone, I can't explain it all, and I am sorry for the pain. I have heard that it is uncomfortable for some..."

"So you never talked to Elijah Craig," Boone interrupted, "sat in the school gym with the gardener, had nightmares about the church exploding, or felt like you were going to throw up all over the floor every time it happened?"

"Nope, that's a gift unique to you. It's pretty cool if you ask me, and once you learn to master it, and just accept that it is as much a part of you as your legs, it won't bother you anymore." Jeff stopped and stared at Boone. "What did you say about the church?"

"It was just another weird daydream. I would find myself in the church with people who were screaming, and then windows were breaking. I don't really know what that had to do with anything."

"I have to get back, and so do you!" Jeff started off toward the suspended bridge.

"Wait!" Boone called to him frustrated. "You can't tell me I *have to* get back. First of all, I don't know why, and second, I can't! Third, and what I really want to know, is how come you can come and go whenever you want?"

Jeff stopped and turned back to Boone. "I guess I do owe you some explanation. I was born here, Boone. My mom and dad were called here for a short season to work. Our family has always been among the garden. It is who we are and who you are too. Many, many years ago, my ancestors were called here, like yours. They worked, they lived, some went back, and some stayed. Those that went back helped start our church with Elijah Craig. They brought him into the garden because he was a man of faith and he was a leader. He met his wife here, an observer. She had been called here as well. But when they went back to their church, they forget the things they had learned. The church started to fall apart. The people were arguing. They were no longer acting as one but as individuals, divided. They became lazy and mean. Half of the group left to return to the Mishpachah to heal so that one-day they would come back and serve. The other half stayed to rebuild what was broken until the others returned. Among the ones to leave was Elijah Craig's wife. This made him so mad that he faked their deaths and made everyone believe that they were buried on the church property. He became angry, so much so that he believed he had to expose the world to the garden. So he tried to enter the garden his own way, leaving clues behind, but he never made it. Something went wrong. We don't really know what, but what I do know is that he had it all wrong. You can't show the world to the garden. The garden has to come out and show itself to the world."

"Sounds like a real jerk to me," Boone said under his breath.

"If he's a jerk, then we all are, Boone. It could happen to any of us. In fact, that is why we have to get back!"

The Jeff in front of him was not the Jeff he thought he knew. It was as if he were looking at someone he had never seen before, someone wiser than himself, someone that he might kind of look up to. "I'm sorry. I mean, I'm sorry you didn't think I would listen."

Jeff shrugged. "All part of my job. Now, we have to go!"

"But I can't! You should know that, something about denying myself."

"Boone, you have to figure that out. I can't help you there. Listen, I'm going back. I'll be waiting for you on the other side."

"What's happening to our church? Is my family okay?" Boone called after him.

Jeff looked over his shoulder and called back, "They're fine, and for now so is our church. Boone, this is much bigger than our small town country church. This is about all of them. We are *one* family Boone Tackett!"

With that, he started his jog down the suspension bridge. When he came to the landing where the bridge met the spiral stairs, he stopped and knelt down as if he were praying. Then he stood back up and started stepping slowly.

What is he doing? He's going to fall off into the garden, Boone worried. To his surprise, the wooden bridge grew like branches from a tree reaching out and stretching their limbs to form the path leading Jeff straight to the falls on the other side of the pennyroyal field. At the falls, the water parted and there in front of Jeff was a door of stone. He turned the knob and went inside without looking back. The bridge grew back as quickly as it had grown outward. "Are you kidding? There really is a door!" Boone said surprised.

Chapter 20

"Did you see that?" Case shouted as he ran back to where Boone was left standing. "It grew…and he walked…and a door. There is a door! We can go home!"

"If the bridge were still there, it would make this a lot easier," Noel mumbled as she joined them.

Boone knew that something important was happening back home, and somehow he was a part of it. Jeff said to accept the voice, so if he really were the 'him' that the voice was referring to, he had to get back. "All right then, what do we need to do?"

Noel pointed to the falls. "We are going out the same way we came in. If there is a door back there, then we are going to find it."

"But Noel, the way out is different for everyone. Say we do find a way over there. Who's to say there is a door for us?"

"Have some faith, old friend," Case crooned. "We won't know unless we try."

"He's right, Boone," Noel whispered. "We have to try. Look at us. Wayne is a mess, Kaylee is homesick, and I am ready to go. I don't know why, but I need to go, now. I have to; I think it's time. You understand, right Boone? I can't stand this anxious feeling inside of me. It's not normal. This is the next step of our journey, Boone. You were right! I am ready to go now. Come on, what do you say?"

Boone knew too well what she was feeling. He also knew that somehow it was up to him to lead them out, but he was curious as to what she was plotting. "I say, what's next? How do we get out?"

"We go through there," she said confidently with her finger pointing clearly at the field of pennyroyal.

"Are you cracked?" Boone nearly shouted. "I just saw her! The woman, she is still healing after what happened. She can't speak or move, and she didn't even get that close. Oh and how can we forget the whole turning into wolves thing?" He thought of Cora, and then Noel, the friend that he cared for so much. "N, I have seen what it can do and so have you! There is a reason it is forbidden!"

"Boone, did you actually see that woman go into the field?" Her voice sounded different. It was softer, intriguing. "None of you went over there, Boone. It wasn't the pennyroyal that made them fall. Remember…it was you." It kind of made sense to Boone, but something about her voice made him uneasy. "With Cora it took several days for the effects of the penny to completely change her, a shorter time for Case and Wayne, but still a few days. So if we move through it fast enough, and concentrate on something else, we should reach the field and be on the other side before anything happens."

"I'm not sure…" he started remembering the sight of the healer, but she abruptly cut him off.

"Well I am! I've studied everything about this place. This is our option," she said emphatically. "I have spent a lot of time studying and researching the pennyroyal. It's okay. Some people back home actually use the stuff as medicine but…"

"But what?" he interrupted.

"But when they used too much is when really bad things would happen. So, we will be fine." Boone studied her carefully. He searched for some sign that she might be falling, but she seemed well. After all, the gardener had told him to let her help him. Maybe this was the moment. Maybe this was what he had to die to. Maybe he had to put aside his own feelings and let her help him. Cora had mentioned to him that the pennyroyal could be overcome by thinking about something else.

He had one more suggestion. "Maybe we should ask the gardener first."

"Enough Boone!" she raised her voice. "Don't you trust me? Look at your sister; she needs her mom and dad! We can't stay here and I can't stand this feeling inside of me. It's like a thousand bees swarming in my stomach and buzzing in my head. It's too much. We have to go now!" Noel lowered her voice. Seeing the concern in Boone, she continued, "We all, even you, need to be at home." He knew exactly what feeling she was describing.

Boone was certain that there had to be another way, but he didn't want to argue with her anymore. She was his best friend and he was hers. He cared about her. She had tried to warn him before his fall, but it was too late. In order to lead this time, he guessed he had better listen. "Okay Keeper, I'll get the others."

"Okay, meet me by the water's edge behind the orchard. I think you know the spot. After we cross the river, we will have to run and run hard. And then, it will all be fine," she glared at him, and then quickly shot him a smile.

He knew the spot and he dreaded going back there. Boone glanced out toward the pennyroyal and then turned back to get his sister. Case, who had been intently listening, went the other direction to help Wayne out of bed.

The cave was dark except for the light glow coming up from the mist that now barely hung over the rivers. The air was calm and filled with the aromas of freshly tilled dirt, ripe cucumbers, and blooming berries. Boone thought about the times he had walked this way before. He thought about the workers on their hands and knees smiling up at him as he scurried by. He remembered the first day he arrived, and the first time his eyes saw the wide expanse of the garden. Wayne leaned on Case for support as he hobbled away. Kaylee followed behind Boone in silence.

Noel waited for them on the bank looking confident and excited. They were all together again. It seemed like months since they had been stranded in the cave. Now they were changed, different. The bonds of friendship that had held them together were altered. There was something new that drew them close, something that allowed them to trust. It was a bond created by the garden. Boone glanced back to see if anyone was looking. He hadn't rehearsed what he would say if the gardener stopped him. Boone patted Wayne on the back as if to say, "I'm here for you this time."

"Well, are you ready?" Noel asked, prepared to lead the charge.

Boone became uneasy; the gardener had said he was supposed to lead them out. "Wait, something is very wrong." The smell of mint was beginning to envelop the air, forcing its way inside him, and wrapping itself around him as if to make him trip and fall.

Noel glared at him. "You have got to be kidding, Boone! You know what? You will always be the same old boring Boone Tackett, won't you? You will keep going after everyone else, just following the crowd. You're not a leader!" With that, she stepped closer to the water. Images of Cora materialized in front of him. He hadn't even said goodbye, or even told her how sorry he was. Now, he found himself in the same situation. Boone lunged toward Noel in the same way he had tried to save Cora, but this time it was too late. By the time he got to her, she had one foot in the water. Noel winked back at him and then stepped in all the way. The mint was thick in the air and made it hard to breath. She was waist high in the water now.

"Look!" Case shouted pointing to Noel, "She was right. Nothing is happening to her. See you on the other side!" Case took a running start and did a cannon ball into the water.

Wayne placed Kaylee's hand in his. "Sorry, but I think we've all been lied to." Boone couldn't believe what he was hearing, not after everything they had just been through.

He watched as his sister and friend inched their way into the water. "This isn't right," he thought. Every part of him was telling him that this was wrong. He couldn't think straight. Boone gagged and gasped for air as the sweet aroma continued its invasion. He hated it, but strangely he craved more. "No!" he told himself. "Try not to breath in too much."

Boone wanted to hear the voice that had guided him to the garden. If the voice really was a product of the gift Jeff spoke of, then it should be clearly telling him that this was a very bad idea. He waited. His friends were more than halfway across the stream. Had they really been tricked? Why? What was so special about this herb that they were forbidden to get near it? He started to feel foggy. It was too late, he had to go after them, if anything to bring them back to heal.

"Leader," the voice of the gardener called to him. The dark complexioned man was actually walking toward him. As Boone stepped into the cool water, his cotton overalls quickly absorbed the liquid around him. Then he heard voices drifting past him in the stream. He had heard them before, in the library that night with Noel. They begged and pleaded for him to stop. The family had now gathered on the shore, but no one jumped in to pull him back as he had done for Cora. Had he gone too far?

His friends had climbed on the bank; Boone was not far behind them. As Boone stepped onto the dry land, he witnessed the most amazing sight he had ever laid eyes on. The pennyroyal glistened like a thousand green emeralds in the dim light of the mist. Its leaves shimmered and swayed with the breeze created from the cascading water of the falls. The others did not seem to be as enamored with this prohibited area. Case, with Kaylee on his back, was off in a sprint. Wayne was doing his best to keep up. Noel, however, was captivated. Her eyes were closed and her arms outstretched. Boone ran to her.

"I've never seen anything like this! Can you smell it, Boone? It's wonderful." Her eyes were glossy. "I think I might even be able to fly!" She had changed; she was different. He couldn't believe he was thinking it, but she kind of looked pretty. Her hair flowed freely down her back absent from its normal ponytail binding. The bright green leaves around them brought out the specks of green in her hazel eyes. "Boone, I…" she started to say something. Then she stared at him intensely and clutched her throat as her body fell to the earth like a wounded animal. He instantly saw what had changed her faith in the garden and created her sudden urge to leave. It was fear of failure, the fear of having almost lost her new friends, and her fear that she had spent too much time studying the pennyroyal.

"Noel!" he screamed. "It wasn't your fault! You couldn't have known!" Then in fierce anger, he pointed across the water at the gardener, and shouted, "You! *You* did this to her! *You* said she would help me! *You* put that responsibility on her. Why are y*ou* taking her from me? *You,* none of *you* even tried to stop us!" On the shore under the branches of the orchard trees, the gardener wept for Boone.

Boone crouched down beside her. "N, wake up! Wake up N! Don't do this! You can fight this! Think about something else. You need to heal. Come on N, we're almost home! Please N! This wasn't your responsibility. It was mine. Don't take this on yourself! We are fine! We're you're friends. I will get us home! I shouldn't have asked you to find a way! I'm sorry! Please come back, Noel! Please!" But she had fallen. Kaylee's screams filled the full air as she tried to run back towards him, and then Boone couldn't hear her anymore.

Boone faced the gardener; he knew this was not about him. This was Noel's choice. She chose this for herself, but he had followed instead of led, and now she was lifeless. "*Deny yourself, Leader.*" Boone thought he was hearing the words of the gardener, but as he concentrated on the voice, he realized that they had come from his own mouth. He had spoken them. One by one the workers fell to their knees in prayer. Noel had said when people left, the garden stopped to say goodbye. He couldn't make out their utterances over the crashing of water. But his words carried through the breeze and straight to his heart, "*Deny.*"

He said it, but he still didn't know what it meant. "Deny what? If I knew what to do, I would have done it by now!" he called back feeling hurt, scared, and angry. Noel's body lay unchanged. Boone eagerly scanned the field hoping to see that others had made it safely to the other side, but like Noel their bodies lay motionless in front of him. "Tell me! I will do anything!"

The falls stopped roaring, the water stopped moving, the workers vanished, and the bodies of his friends faded into the plants around him. He looked to the shore, and then back to find that he was face to face with the gardener.

"Will you do anything, Leader?" the gardener's asked. "Deny yourself, Leader!"

"Where did they go? What did you do to them?"

"This isn't about me, son. This is about you, you know that, don't you?" His voice was no longer jovial but firm. His face shown unyielding under the straw hat he always wore. Boone waited for that cordial smile that had once prayed over him and welcomed him, but it never came. "Deny yourself!"

"But I don't have anything, I don't even know who I am anymore! I'm afraid!" he cried. "Don't you see that?"

The gardener raised his eyebrows solemnly at Boone. "Well, I guess you do have something then, don't you, Leader? You have a choice to make."

"But what if I make the wrong choice? Will we all die?"

"Deny yourself!" the gardener shouted. A large crack resonated in the cave, the water rushed again, and the bodies of his friends reappeared. With tears still in his eyes, the gardener was back on the opposite side calling out instructions to Boone.

It was as if he had been there all along, and the dialog between them had never happened.

"Deny yourself," he repeated. Boone kneeled down by Noel's stiff body. His head ached. The overwhelming aroma pulled him deeper into worry, doubt, and fear. He feared he would fail, feared that the pain he felt would eventually lead to his death. He feared what it would feel like to lose his friends. "Deny," he thought again. Putting one arm under Noel's bent legs and another under her neck, he reached down and lifted her up. The weight of her body pulled down on him. He trudged through the pennyroyal to the far back where the field rested at the base of the falls' river. Then he went back. Although the smell brought him close to throwing up, he lifted his friends one by one as pain seared throughout his body and pulsated in his head. *Deny the pain of your labor,* he thought. The words continued to spread through him, billowing out straight from his heart to the place where he had invited salvation to live long ago, that place he had pushed aside, forgotten about, and kept to himself. He knew the purpose of this moment and he knew what he had to deny. It wasn't a voice that was pushing him; it was his center, his compass.

His sister was last. He lifted her in his arms, hoping to lift her far above the attacking fragrance of the field. He knew that if he let her go she would never make it home. The pain coursing through him reminded Boone that it had not gone away, but this wasn't about him. It was about her. It didn't matter how he felt as long as she was safe. He pressed forward trying to do as Cora had instructed. He thought about the time Kaylee had asked to bring him to class for show and tell, and the Christmases decorating the tree together. He remembered how he had almost lost her in the river.

He was close to the edge when a new voice spoke to him; a voice so dark and absent from life that it startled him and caused him to fall to his knees with Kaylee still firm in his grasp. "A leader, is that what you think we are? Is that what they told you? You shouldn't have started looking for this place. It doesn't

186

suit us. Look at us." Boone turned to see where the voice was coming from. "Your arms are weak, aren't they? Like your will," the voice hissed and cackled. "Like us, Boone."

"Show yourself! Who are you?" Boone screamed.

The pennyroyal parted as an icy wind blew through Boone. He could faintly see the figure of a boy making itself clearer to him. With a second gust of wind Boone instantly stood head on with a very dark version of himself. "You know, this poor, humble, isolated plant has a really nice smell," the eerie voice taunted Boone with a wry smile. "You like it too, don't you? The gardener knew you would. Why else didn't he want you around it? This is their secret you know. Maybe it's worth something. I wonder how it tastes. Why else do they want people to leave? No one stays here forever. Right? You do the work and then you leave! Don't you see? They get what they want from you, and then they tell you to go. Everything seems so perfect, they are all so happy. But here you are in pain, sick, and all alone. We need to stick together Boone, you and me. I won't ever leave you."

Boone's arms began to weaken again and the nausea in his stomach returned. Terrified of what he saw, his body shook with fear. The voice of the gardener rung clearly, "Deny yourself, Leader!"

"I'm not afraid of you!" Boone shouted to his image.

"Oh really! Then why are you standing in the middle of this living death?" His reflection circled around him. "You are no leader. Go back to your *church*, sit on the front row, and keep your mouth shut! That's what you are good at! You were happier then. Life was easy, so easy. It was safe there. Right, Boone? You messed with it, and now you are going to die. Your friends don't even like you now! You are a FAILURE!" Its words softened, "There is a way to make it all go away, all of it. Stay with me and we can go back to the way things were. We can do this, just us."

Boone tried hard to turn away, but a stab of pain at the back of his neck forced his eyes to roll back in his head. "You are afraid of change! You're weak! You are nothing without me!" It had been true. Boone had once believed that it was all true, but not anymore. It wasn't who he was now. He was different. He had changed. The garden had changed him. His image ranted on with his cruel tirade. It reminded him of every failure in his life, of every time he cried in pain, or every time he had ever been afraid of anything. It circled around him taunting and preying on his soul. "You saw her turning, didn't you? You pretended that you didn't, but you saw her fear. You didn't want to see the signs, did you? She knew the risks. She believed she was strong enough, but you...you knew she was wrong. You were afraid to lead her. If you failed, she would know. You let her down too many times, how could you do it again? She was your best friend. How selfish of you Boone to try to deny me! You have always had me! I have always been here! I am you!"

Boone closed his eyes and screamed, "No! It's not true. This is not the person I want to be! It is not who I am! Take my life if it will save my friends. Oh God, I'm sorry! Do your will with my life! Deliver me from me!"

Chapter 21

Boone felt hands under his shoulders, back, and legs moving him. "I'm here, Bubby," he heard his sister whisper. "You did it, Bubby! You made it all better. I don't feel bad anymore. We are here. Please wake up. Please see that everything is okay. Don't worry. They won't drop you." Boone cracked open an eye slowly to see that it was not workers in the garden who were lifting him, but his friends. The crashing of the falls was louder than before as they carried him to a dry area beside the base of the waterfalls. They had made it, all of them. The glowing mist still hung heavy in the air, but the smell was clean and crisp.

"Thank you," he said, not knowing which of his friends would hear it. They gently set him down and walked away.

"No, thank you. We'll wait for you," Noel assured sitting to rest not far from him. Boone staggered to his feet and stepped back to the edge of the place where the water met the shore. From here, the pennyroyal appeared withered and useless. It no longer held the same intrigue as it had before. Across the field, he saw workers holding their hands high in the air as they joyfully cheered and shouted praise.

Looking back one last time, Boone saw the gardener with his hands on his heart and tears still lingering in his eyes. Boone closed his eyes and listened. "You denied that part of you that was doubt, fear, and worry. That part that fed on your selfish desires. Even in your pain you would not let your sister fall. You died to yourself, Boone Tackett. Now it is time to go out into the world and lead." Boone opened his eyes and smiled at the gardener. The gardener took off his hat and waved goodbye.

Now on their feet, the others were alert and looking at Boone. They did not ask questions, but he knew they were looking for him to lead them home. He knew that he could never truly explain how he was changed. He would try, but they would have to experience self-denial in their own way. For all he knew, they may have already. He also knew that now he could truly lead them.

"So now what?" Case asked Noel.

"I don't know," she replied with a smile.

"What do you mean you don't know?" he questioned sarcastically. "You know everything."

"Apparently not, at least not this time," she smiled turning to Boone. "Right, Leader?"

Boone lifted his right hand, closed his eyes and cleared his confusion of everything but home. The others gasped as the waterfall split in two, revealing a very large wooden door. On the door was the symbol of the tree of life. Boone wasn't surprised. This was his door. It was the way he had learned to lead them home.

"Are you serious?" Wayne protested. "Leaders get magic powers! That is so unfair!"

"First of all, I don't have *magical* powers," Boone said reaching up toward the golden door handle. "Second, it's not about fair. It's about faith." As he gave the handle an easy pull, the door swung open slowly revealing a brilliant white pathway. "Well, this is it." Boone stepped confidently through the doorway and onto the path before him. The others followed willingly, not questioning his judgment.

Once everyone had stepped onto the path, the door behind them shut and another appeared immediately in front of them. Boone recognized it instantaneously. With his center assuring him, he flung it open and rushed through without looking back.

He was welcomed by a smell that was warm and familiar, like musty books and newly polished hardwood. The others hurried in trusting Boone to lead them. The door behind them shut. Cheers broke out among the five as they hugged him and each other. "You did it, Bubby!" Kaylee squealed.

"I don't know what to say, B," Wayne started.

"We could have died, but you led us home." Case extended his hand; Boone happily shook it.

"Boone, he's right. I don't know what you did back there, but if it weren't for you," Noel said holding back tears. "If it weren't for you, we…"

He stopped her. "It's not about me, but thanks." Boone felt like a celebrity among the few that knew him the best. He knew that they would each remember the trials they had faced, but they would never need to remind each other of them again. They would only need to encourage one another on where they had learned to succeed.

"I knew you would find the way, Boone Tackett," Jeff spoke from the front of the sanctuary. Boone walked towards him. Jeff embraced Boone like a brother who had been searching a long time for a missing family member. Then, Jeff took a piece of paper from his pocket and handed it to Kaylee. She recognized the note she had once written and left on the front pew. Smiling, he said, "I don't think your parents will need this now."

"Thank you," was all that Boone could say. The agitated screech of the Sunday school bell announced the end of Sunday school and the beginning of worship. They were all dressed exactly as they were the day the earth had fallen through the church graveyard. Boone's jeans were no longer muddy and wet.

Kaylee was the sight of flawlessness in her neatly pressed dress. Noel's hair had returned to its ponytail and her floral backpack rested on her shoulders. Boone was actually startled to see Wayne and Case in something other than their assigned garden attire. No one physically bore the markings of their mission, but Boone knew what they were and who they had become as a result of the happenings within the Mishpachah. It was written in their smiles and their laughter, in the joy they did not have before.

"Mommy!" Kaylee squealed at the sight of her mother. She ran to her and hugged her tightly. "I've missed you so much!"

"Well, sweetie, I have missed you too. How was Sunday school?" Mrs. Tackett inquired.

Boone immediately recognized that no one knew they were gone. They had come back before he had even left for the cemetery that rainy Sunday morning. Everything was as it had been before he left…except for him.

As congregation members made their way into the sanctuary, the others quickly took their seats at the front of the church. Boone was about to sit down when Jeff's grandmother walked up to him with a grin. She smelled of lavender and chamomile. It was a smell that made him feel safe. He didn't think he had ever seen her smile before. Maybe she had, but he hadn't paid attention until this moment. "Good morning Leader," she nodded. Then walking to where she had played the organ every Sunday since he was a child, she sat down and began to play.

Boone sat beside Noel and Jeff sat on the other side of her. She leaned over and whispered, "Boone Tackett, you truly are not ordinary anymore."

He glanced at the red book peeking out of her backpack. "I would have to agree with you."

1 year later...

Boone's seat was in the front row of the Great Crossing Baptist Church. He let his mind stray as he looked around the room at the comfortably familiar contrast of the red carpet and white pews. This Sunday, the sunlight poured through the stained glass windows reminding him of the events that occurred a year ago on a similar autumn day. He waited patiently for Wayne who had volunteered to help his dad fix the broken air conditioner in the church basement.

The room was exceptionally hot. Several rows behind him, a few ladies were fanning themselves so fast with their paper fans that Boone tossed around the image of them flying away and getting trapped in the chandelier. He couldn't help it. It made for a funny mental picture. "Hey Boone," the voice of his best friend Noel called to him, "scoot over. Jeff is sitting with us today."

"Doesn't he always sit with us?" Boone asked sarcastically.

Noel blushed. She and Jeff had spent the rest of their eighth grade year and the following summer sorting through the books in the hidden library together. Boone couldn't quite understand how they found fun in reading and re-reading old books. Truth be told, he knew they had a fondness for each other. Now that they were in high school, he thought it was time that they both admitted it, but he hadn't been able to convince either one of them of their mutual mindsets.

As the two squeezed in, Boone's younger sister Kaylee joined them. Noticeably, she put her hair behind her ears to show off new magnetic earrings. "She thinks they're real," he whispered to Noel.

"I like them," Noel said winking at her.

"It's going to get hotter," Wayne shot up from behind him. An elderly gentleman in jeans and a worn out t-shirt was seated beside him. Wayne's dad had been coming to church for about a month. He said it was because Wayne was suddenly behaving and doing twice the amount of work around the farm that he was told to do. He wanted to know, as he said, 'What are they teaching kids in church these days?' In many ways, Wayne's dad reminded Boone of the gardener. He worked hard, only spoke when he had something that he believed needed to be heard, and loved his family completely. Boone missed the gardener and the Mishpachah. There wasn't a day that passed that he didn't go over every moment of it.

He had returned with big ideas and bigger plans. He had undergone a transformation from being an ordinary church sitter to a recognizable leader. Because of it, he persuaded his cousin Case to join the choir, started a prayer group at the middle school, and often asked Reed if he could give testimonies to the other youth. He never spoke of the garden as if it was a real place, but he passed on lessons he learned during his time in the Mishpachah as if he had learned them through every day life, but something had happened as the months passed. The excitement and newness of his changed life meshed into his everyday. The final Sunday school bell chimed jarring him from his musing and announcing that service would start shortly. It was a definite improvement from the *BZZZZSCHRING* of the old one.

Jeff's grandmother approached the organ, took her seat, and began playing a melody of older church hymns while last minute attendees located seats toward the back of the sanctuary. Case stepped up on the stage with his guitar and a huge grin. It made Boone proud to see him up there. Case welcomed churchgoers to service, and after asking them to stand; he led the singing of a series of more contemporary worship songs. Boone was still amazed at the variation Case had been able to make in worship. At first, the change had been a point of contention in the church. Initially, Case took it upon himself, with some advice from Noel's dad, to work in the acoustic version of a few songs still found in the cloth bound church hymnal. The mix brought a peaceful compromise between the generations. As Case sang, Boone could not refrain from lifting his hands. There was a release, a new freedom of thankfulness that had consumed him. His worship was no longer a time to dream about what he was having for lunch that afternoon, or how he was going to pass Math, but rather a time to be thankful for the good things that hadn't happened yet. Though the past few months had been quiet, he sensed without sickness – he had learned to control that – and after his talk with Jeff, that a spiritual storm was brewing that would affect everyone around them.

The sermon was about Joseph's interpretation of Pharaoh's cupbearer's dream, and how the cupbearer forgot all about Joseph after he was restored to his position. Boone was tempted to count the number of iron spindles on the balcony railing, or allow his mind to imagine Joseph in his coat of many colors walking around the Mishpachah. He found that by taking notes he usually was able to keep his eyes from wandering and focus more on the teaching. It never failed that Jeff's dad would slip in something that those who had a connection with the garden would know about. Boone did not feel it was time to share with his parents about his journey. Although, the changes in him were more than evident, he had a new perspective that touched every aspect of his life. So much so, that he managed to keep his room neat. It wasn't exactly clean, but it was neat.

As the morning's rituals were drawing near to a close, Jeff came to the stage. Recently, he had started making the church announcements. This was another one of their youth director Reed's ideas to incorporate the youth into the service and give them a presence among the congregation. It was important to him that the older church members saw them as a functioning part of the church body. He claimed the verse that said, 'Don't let anyone look down on you because you are young' as his life motto.

"On Saturday we'll be having a back to school party for the youth," Jeff started. "Don't forget to bring a friend. If you are interested in being in this year's Christmas musical, practices are beginning this month and you can see Case or Mr. Peterson after church today. This morning . . ." Jeff paused his announcement and gave Boone a goofy smile. Boone tried to read his expression, and mouthed the word 'what'. Jeff continued, "We would like to welcome a new family. They have recently moved here and are joining the fellowship from the Southland Community Church."

Boone Tackett craned his head to see the family of four walking up the aisle of the church. The father and mother were vaguely familiar to him. The shorter of their two children he absolutely knew he had seen somewhere. He could make out that the taller of the two was a girl, but he couldn't see her face through the standing attendees. When the family reached the front, Noel grabbed Boone's knee so hard that he kicked the seat in front of him. Watching her gaze, he immediately saw what caught her eye. He swallowed hard and, for a second, lost his breath as the mystery girl's face became clearly visible.

"Let me introduce to you," Jeff said, "the Thornton's, David, Melissa, Cole, and Cora." Boon hadn't forgotten for a minute what she looked like. Her brown hair hung in long soft curls, and her green eyes glittered under the light of the chandelier. "Let's welcome them to our family." Church members left their pews to hug the new members and introduce themselves.

"Go," Noel nudged him.

"I can't. We never talked about it. I haven't . . .." Boone stuttered.

"I know you were never able to tell her that you were sorry for what happened, but you are going to have to talk to her sooner or later," Noel encouraged. "Just go and at least say, 'hi'.

Maybe she won't remember you and you can start over. Who knows how the whole garden transfer to the world thing works."

"Okay, but you are going with me."

"Sure thing, Leader," she whispered.

Boone's seat was not quite ten feet from where Cora stood with her family, but the walk there felt like miles. He came to her father first who shook Boone's hand with a kind firmness that said, "Good to see you again." Her mother hugged him, as did her brother.

"Leader, I mean . . . Boone," Cora spoke first, "we must talk, right away!"

Without warning a large cloud descended over the church and the room was cloaked in darkness. A loud commotion bellowed outside. There was a roar followed by a pounding on the glass. Instantly, the room went still. The entire congregation, with the exception of those who had been to or knew of the garden, was frozen in time. Then, the noise grew louder. Boone saw the shadows of people outside. Their fists came down hard on the glass, voices wailed and cried out painfully. Boone looked at Cora for some sort of explanation as to what was happening.

"We must go," she mouthed. He grabbed her hand and practically pulled her back down the aisle. Jeff, Noel, Case, and Wayne followed close behind. Boone threw open the church door. He held it open as a strong wind tried to force it shut.

"Hurry," he shouted to his friends. The wind picked up speed making it hard to keep the door open. The pounding grew louder and shook the walls of the church building. Jeff helped Boone grip the door to allow the others through first.

"Hey Leader," Jeff called to Boone.

"Let me guess," Boone yelled back, "it's time!" Then, the door slammed shut behind them.

The Books of the Gardener

Boone: The Ordinary
Boone: The Forgotten
Boone: The Sanctified

Orlo: The Created
Orlo: The Burdened
Orlo: The Chosen

Lewis: The Wounded
Lewis: The Scarred
Lewis: The Beloved

The Book of the Gardener

For more information on The Books of the Gardener visit:
www.TheBooksOfTheGardener.com